Loyalty
TO A
GANGSTA?

JOHN L. ROSE

Good2Go Publishing

LOYALTY TO A GANGSTA 2

Written by John L. Rose

Cover Design: Davida Baldwin

Typesetter: Mychea

ISBN: 9781947340046

Copyright © 2018 Good2Go Publishing

Published 2018 by Good2Go Publishing

7311 W. Glass Lane • Laveen, AZ 85339

www.good2gopublishing.com

https://twitter.com/good2gobooks

G2G@good2gopublishing.com

www.facebook.com/good2gopublishing

www.instagram.com/good2gopublishing

DEDICATION

To my Heavenly Father who is first in my life; my mom . . . I love you for life; and to my pops, I love you with that forever type of love, my dude!

Last but not least, Ray Brown. You my dude, and I thank you greatly. We in it til the wheels fall off and the engine drops out of this mutha! You get my vibe! Love!

ACKNOWLEDGMENTS

This book is for my family and fans! Sorry for the wait, but we back! Ride with the boy!

Loyalty
TO A
GANGSTA 2

PROLOGUE

A Year and Three Months Earlier

"Do you remember the story we told you, Brianna, about how your father died?"

"Of course!"

"Well, we never told you that we knew who the killer was!"

"What?" Brianna yelled, looking over to her mother. "Is Darrell telling the truth?"

Victoria nodded her head yes.

"The same person that murdered your father, honey, is now locked up in a federal prison; but he is soon to be released in two years, and he's coming here!"

"He's after you two, isn't he?" Gabe spoke up asking Victoria but looking from her to Darrell and then back to her.

"Actually, Gabriel," Victoria began as she sat forward in her seat, "he's after not only myself and Darrell, but also Brianna."

"Why me?" she asked.

Victoria began to explain to Brianna and Gabe

how she and Darrell were the ones who were responsible for getting Brianna's father's killer locked up after setting him up and allowing the FBI to catch him in the middle of a cocaine buy.

"Wait!" Brianna spoke up after Victoria paused. "You say this person that killed my father was into buying cocaine?"

"Yes, sweetheart!" Victoria answered.

"But I thought my father was into robbing? Why would he have any dealings buying coke? I don't understand, Momma!"

Victoria sighed as she looked over at her husband and then continued.

"Brianna, sweetie! Your father really wasn't into robbing. We only told you that to keep you away from this same lifestyle that you're already in. Your father was a very large cocaine distributor, and the same person who murdered him is or was your father's business partner!"

Gabe saw the expression on Brianna's face and reached over and gripped her hand.

"So, let me get this clear," Gabe said. "This person that's due to be released in two years, you say that he's after Brianna as well as the both of you. So, basically, I'm being trained to protect the three of you?"

"No!" Darrell spoke up again. "You two don't know it, but Lorenzo is around for the reason of protecting me and mostly Victoria. You're the one we've decided will protect Brianna, and seeing as though you two are now engaged, we figured you'd do whatever it takes to protect her and keep her safe."

Gabe nodded his head after listening to Darrell. He then shifted his eyes over to George and Trinity.

"I'm aware of what George Warren can do, but what about the white girl? What can you do, Trinity?"

"Be careful, Gabriel!" Victoria told him with a smile. "You may not know who Trinity is, but if you pull her up on the internet you'll see what she's known for."

"How about somebody tell me!" Gabe requested, looking back over at Trinity.

"Trinity is the best mixed martial arts fighter in the world. She knows more than sixteen different fighting styles," Darrell explained to Gabe.

"And you're going to teach me all these styles?" Gabe asked as he looked back over at Trinity.

"I will attempt to teach you three styles to use," Trinity told him. "After seeing your ability with your hands, I can see you've fought already. Who showed you how to box?"

"My mother's father!" Gabe answered. "So, a'ight! We know the truth, so when does this training start?"

"You leave Monday morning, Gabriel," Darrell informed him.

"Whoa! What did you say?" Brianna asked, raising her voice. "What do you mean he's leaving? Where is my fiancé going?"

"We're leaving for Tokyo on Monday morning at 6:30 a.m.," Trinity spoke up.

"Naw!" Brianna interrupted. "Hell no! Y'all not taking my man across the fucking world to train him!"

"Bri, relax, ma!" Gabe told her, only for her to go off on him and refuse for him to go.

He leaned over and whispered into her ear a few moments. Gabe then pulled back and met her eyes.

"Do you trust me?"

Brianna slowly shook her head, hating what he was asking her. She rolled her eyes and looked back over at Trinity.

"How long are you keeping him over there?"

"Depends on how fast a learner he is!" George answered this time. "I'll also be training Gabriel, so it can take from six to twelve months for him to really properly learn what he's being taught!"

"I can't believe this shit!" Brianna said, rolling her eyes in disgust.

Gabe watched Brianna for a few moments, until she looked back at him and gave him a look before taking his hand into hers. Gabe then winked at her and looked back at Darrell and Victoria.

"We'll see you guys come Monday!"

CHAPTER 1

Present Day

B rianna was aggravated and unable to get any real sleep, only to hear the ringing of the cell phone right next to her head. She growled as she opened her eyes and first looked over at the bedside clock. It was 8:15 a.m. and her phone was already ringing. She picked up the Samsung Galaxy S9 and answered without even checking to see who was calling.

"What?" she said into the phone after picking up.

"Brianna, we got problems!"

"I'm not surprised!" she replied after hearing what Sherry had said.

She threw the blanket off of her while listening to her girl explain the new problems concerning Jit Jit getting arrested.

Hanging up with Sherry after telling her that she was on her way to the spot, Brianna then took a ten-minute shower and then dried out. While she headed into her bedroom to put on a pair of panties, the phone began to ring again.

"This same bullshit!" she cursed as she snatched up the Galaxy from the bed. "What the hell?"

"Brianna!"

Recognizing her step-father's voice, Brianna replied, "What is it, Darrell?"

"You okay, baby girl?"

"Actually, I'm not!" she told him truthfully. "It's eight o'clock in the damn morning and I'm getting calls about my people getting arrested, and now I've gotta drive way the hell out to the city to deal with this new bullshit!"

"Brianna, calm down!" Darrell told her. "You can-not let your—!"

"Darrell, I'm kind of in a hurry!" Brianna interrupted her step-father. "You called for a reason?"

"I tell you what, Brianna!" Darrell began, sighing loudly. "I have something for you, but I will just have Lorenzo bring it to you. Hopefully, your mood will change once you receive what I'm sending you."

"Yeah, whatever!" Brianna stated as she hung up the phone right afterward.

~ ~ ~

Brianna was to meet the two bodyguards that were assigned to her by Darrell and her fiancé before he left on his training trip across the damn globe. She ignored both of their asses as she walked through the parking garage and straight to the recently purchased 2018 model GLS 450 Benz truck.

Once inside the truck, Brianna spied her two bodyguards rushing to get into the navy-blue Range Rover they used to follow behind her. She wasted no time starting the Benz and was flying out of the garage leaving her bodyguards behind. She dug out her cell phone and pulled up Sherry's number and called her girl.

"Hello!" Sherry answered in the middle of the second ring.

"Sherry, this is Brianna! Y'all still at the spot, right?"

"Yeah, girl! It's me, Tamara, and Jit Jit right now!"

"I should be there in fifteen minutes," Brianna told her as she looked in the rearview mirror and spotted the Range Rover a few hundred feet behind her.

Immediately after hanging up with Sherry, her cell phone rang again. She answered the call without checking to see who was calling her.

3

"What?"

"What's up with you?"

Brianna recognized the voice, but she still glanced down at the screen to see that it was her ex-boyfriend, Anthony, calling. Brianna went off.

"What the hell did I tell your ass, Anthony? Why the hell are you calling me?"

"What?"

"What!" Brianna repeated. "Nigga, what the fuck you mean 'what'? I already told you not to call me no damn more!"

"So, that's it then?" he asked. "So what happened between us wasn't—?"

"Nigga, I just needed to bust a nut and I let you eat my pussy! It's over with and really shouldn't have happened. So, for the last time, do not call me again!"

After hanging up in Anthony's face while he was still trying to talk, Brianna tossed the phone into the center console as she was turning down the street that Jit Jit's spot was on that he ran for her with his young team.

Brianna saw Sherry and Jit Jit stepping out of the trap house, and she spied Jit Jit light up a blunt. She pulled the Benz up in front of the spot and parked behind Sherry's new 2018 Infiniti QX80.

"Where's everybody at?" Brianna asked as soon as she climbed from the truck as both Sherry and Jit Jit walked up to meet her.

"Tamara just left to drive up to the store, and I sent the team home," Sherry explained to Brianna. "I don't think it's a good idea to crank things up just yet!"

"What exactly happened?" Brianna asked, looking straight at Jit Jit.

She listened to him as he began explaining how an Officer Jones had been tripping and sweating the spot. The officer caught him early that morning on the way to the spot and planted a half ounce of weed on him.

"Wait! You say he planted an ounce of weed on you?" Brianna interrupted.

"Yeah!" Jit Jit answered, but then quickly added, "Just let me finish though!"

"Alright, go ahead!" Brianna told him as she folded her arms across her chest while balling up her face.

"This crab-ass officer had one inside the back of

5

his patrol car, and while we were headed downtown, he asked me how long I had been working for you."

"Wait!" Brianna started.

"Brianna, just let him finish telling you the story!" Sherry spoke up.

"Alright, alright! Finish!" Brianna ordered, waving her hand for Jit Jit to continue with his story.

"Well after he asked me that shit and I wouldn't answer his question, homeboy kept on talking!" Jit Jit told Brianna.

Jit Jit further explained, in so many words, that the officer wanted him to let Brianna know that she had a decision to make to either do business or be dealt with.

"Do business or be dealt with? What?" "Brianna repeated with a very confused look on her face.

"I only know that there's been word out that some new team in Overtown and a few other areas are pushing some new shit, and niggas are getting at them since their shit is crazy cheaper than what we been getting rid of our shit for!" Jit Jit explained.

"Jit Jit's not the only one that's been complaining about this same issue, Brianna!" Sherry spoke up again, just as Tamara was pulling up.

Brianna looked over at Tamara as her girl was parking, and then focused back on Jit Jit and Sherry. She sighed deeply and loudly as she tried to figure out what was going on and wondering who this so-called new team was.

"What's up, Brianna, girl?" Tamara said as she walked up to Brianna and the others. "How long you been here?"

"A few minutes," Brianna replied as she watched Tamara hand Jit Jit a bag from Burger King and then a tall orange juice to Sherry.

"So, Jit Jit and Sherry told you what's been going on?" Tamara asked as she opened a soft pack of Newports, just as she noticed Lorenzo's new 2018 model Lexus LS500 slowly pulling up the street. "Here comes Lorenzo, y'all!"

Brianna looked back to see Lorenzo's Lexus just as it pulled up in front of them and parked on the street. She turned her attention back to Jit Jit.

"Jit Jit, listen! I want you to find—!"

"Oh my God!" Sherry and Tamara said in unison, with Sherry dropping her drink.

Brianna looked down at the juice that Sherry had just dropped and then looked back up into the two girls' faces as they stared out toward the street.

Brianna then turned to see what they were staring at, only to freeze once her eyes locked onto the familiar face that stood only a few feet away from her and smirking.

"Yeah, ma! It's me, beautiful!" Gabe stated as Brianna took off rushing toward his open arms.

Brianna was fully crying by the time she was in her man's arms, hugging him tightly as she buried her face into his muscular chest. She cried harder after feeling his arms wrap tightly around her.

Sherry smiled as she and the others stood and stared as Brianna and Gabe embraced. She couldn't help looking over Gabe's now even better looking muscular and toned five-foot-ten, 215-pound frame. He had on a pair of black metallic jeans, a white wifebeater, and a pair of white-on-black Air Max.

"Damn, his ass is even sexier than before he left!" Tamara said, smiling as she also looked over Gabe.

"The pretty boy muthafucker still looks the exact same to me! I just can't see why Brianna's still wasting her time with this clown!" Jit Jit scoffed with a lot of attitude while sucking his teeth.

"Cool out, youngin!" Lorenzo warned Jit Jit, smiling as he shook his head at the young gangsta.

8

CHAPTER 2

G abe was happy to be back home and kicking it
with Brianna and the rest of her team, who
were also his friends. He hung out at the trap house
with the crew and answered a few questions before
he noticed how Brianna made sure she was standing
right next to him or touching his arm or back. He
allowed her touch since he already had heard how
she was acting lately with everyone. He knew it was
because he had been gone longer than the planned
year that he was supposed to be away.

"Boy, I'm still tripping how big yo' ass got,
Gabe!" Sherry started, smiling as she stood to the
right of him, still looking him over in approval of
what she saw.

"His ass is sexy!" Tamara stated, also smiling at
him.

"Don't you hoes get hurt!" Brianna said,
shooting both her girls a look, which caused them to
laugh out loud.

"Seriously though, Gabe!" Sherry said as she
changed her tone. "We're happy you back 'cause
Brianna was driving us crazy! What took you so long

to come back though?"

"I wanted to go over a few more things to add to what I was being taught," Gabe admitted, but then looked to his right and met Brianna's eyes. "What's going on, Bri?"

"What?" she asked in confusion at the question. "What are you talking about?"

"I saw the look on your face when we drove up," he told her. "What's the problem?"

Brianna ran her hand back through her hair and sighed. "Babe, I really don't know what's going on. Jit Jit and Sherry were just telling me about some new team that's out there and are warning me that I can either do business with them or be dealt with."

"Do business or be dealt with, huh?" Gabe repeated with a small smirk on his face. "So, who's this new team?"

"That's just it, boo!" Sherry chimed in. "We don't know! Jit Jit just got the message today when he got arrested this morning."

"Tell me about it!" Gabe stated, looking straight at Jit Jit.

~ ~ ~

After hearing Jit Jit's story, with the help of

Tamara and Sherry, Gabe looked over at Lorenzo.

"Bruh, let me hold ya keys."

"Gabe, where are you about to go?" Brianna asked, watching as Lorenzo handed over his car keys.

"Getting some answers!" Gabe answered Brianna before looking over at Lorenzo and saying, "Stay close to Brianna until I get back up with y'all!"

"I got it, lil bruh!" Lorenzo responded as Gabe turned back around and kissed Brianna on the lips before he whispered something in her ear that stopped the question she was about to ask him.

Brianna watched Gabe turn and walk out of the house. She then turned and looked at Lorenzo.

"Zoe, go with him!"

Lorenzo shook his head and said, "No! Trust me, Brianna. Gabe's good by himself. He ain't the same kid he was before he left a year ago!"

"His ass damn sure don't look like it either!" Tamara said as she and Sherry high-fived each other and chuckled.

~ ~ ~

"I'ma see you later, Momma!" Melody told her mother as the two of them stepped out of her mother's house and onto the front porch.

She hugged and then kissed her mother on the cheek before walking out to the new Kia Stinger AWD that her fiancé had bought her.

Melody hit the key remote to her car, unlocked the car doors, and was just walking around to the driver's door when she noticed the new model Lexus that was slowly pulling up alongside her.

Melody watched the window begin to slide down, just as she was reaching for her car door, when she heard a familiar voice.

"What's up, Miss Lady?"

Melody looked back over at the Lexus, and her mouth dropped open as she stared in disbelief.

"Oh my God!" she cried as she stood watching Gabe climb out of the car.

She let out a loud scream as she took off racing around her car and throwing herself up onto Gabe. She wrapped her arms around his neck.

"Oh my God!" Melody cried again, smiling as she pulled back to meet his eyes that she truly missed. "Gabe, it's really you, boy?"

"Yeah, it's me, cutey!" Gabe replied, showing off his famous smirk. "You look good, shorty."

"I was just thinking the same thing about you,

boy!" Melody told him as she looked him over. "Boy, look at you!"

Gabe laughed after Melody threw her arms back around him again and hugged him tight. He gave her her moment.

"So, how you been doing?" he asked.

"I've been great, Gabe. But where have you been?" she asked. "I asked Duke where you went to, and he didn't know either. He just told me that you left to handle something with that girl you got engaged to before you just disappeared."

"Where is Duke?" Gabe asked.

"His ass is at home!" Melody explained. "We got a place together now after we got engaged!"

Gabe saw the diamond ring on her finger that she held up for him to inspect. He immediately congratulated her with a big hug.

"Let me guess!" Melody said after her good news was out. "You wanna see your boy, don't ya?"

Melody saw the smile on his face that she loved and missed so much. She then shook her head side to side and smiled back at Gabe before telling him to follow her back to her and Duke's new place.

~ ~ ~

13

Gabe followed Melody from her mother's house to Aventura, where he pulled in through the front security gates at the high-rise apartment building. He then followed her around to the front entrance of the parking garage.

Gabe parked the Lexus beside Melody's car, hit the locks once he got out, and then walked over to meet up with her as she was walking around the back end of her Kia.

"This is where y'all live at now, huh?" he asked as he and Melody headed toward the elevator.

"We just moved in about three months ago," Melody informed Gabe as the two of them stepped into the elevator. She hit the call button as she continued talking. "So, how are you and that girl you got into the engagement with doing?"

"We good!" Gabe answered as they stepped onto the elevator. "She was happy as hell to see me when I got back!"

They continued their conversation as they rode the elevator up to the twelfth floor. Melody stepped off with Gabe right behind her. She led the way to the front door of her apartment and wasn't surprised to hear the music from inside playing loud as always.

She unlocked and opened up the front door, stepped inside, and saw Boo Man walking out of the kitchen with a big bowl of cheese puffs.

"Melody, what's—? Oh shit!" Boo Man stopped in mid-sentence after seeing homeboy that walked into the apartment behind Melody, who he instantly recognized as his friend. "Gabe, what the fuck?"

Gabe laughed as his homie rushed past Melody and handed off the bowl to her, right before he wrapped him up in a big bear hug. Gabe then peeped Duke and then his nigga, Silk, walking into the front room after leaving the den.

"Oh shit!" Duke said after seeing Ace and then taking off and rushing toward his boy after Boo Man had released him.

"My G!" Duke called out as he ran over and embraced Gabe.

Duke released Gabe and looked his boy over.

"Damn, nigga! Fuck you been at? You done got big as hell, fam!"

Duke expected Gabe to say something, but he noticed the direction that his main man's eyes were directed. Duke looked back to see not only Silk but also his sister, Shantae, standing a few feet away

15

staring back.

"My G, listen!"

"Naw!" Gabe interrupted, showing his smile. "It's cool, playboy! Everything good!"

Duke decided to let the ongoing issue remain on a silent hold for the moment as he led his boy into the den.

"So, what's good, my nigga?" Duke asked once everyone was crowded into the den and the music was turned off. "Where the fuck you been all this time?"

"Ain't nobody tell you after I left?" Gabe asked. "I told Brianna to let you know what was up!"

"Naw, my dude!" Duke stated. "Ain't nobody told me shit! Matter of fact, I ain't seen ya lady since you up and disappeared. Y'all still kicking it, right?"

Gabe shifted his eyes over to Shantae before he realized it, only to find her eyes locked back onto his. He then noticed the change in her looks and could see that she had filled out. Her body was now five foot six, 34C-23-40, and with a slim and athletic but curvy build. Gabe broke their eye contact and changed the conversation.

"Fam, you still doing your thing?"

"No doubt!" Duke answered as he began smiling at his boy. "What's up? You trying to get back to work?"

"We'll talk about that!" Gabe told him. "I'm trying to figure out some information about some new team out and around hustling. You heard anything?"

"What you wanna know?" Shantae asked, speaking up and drawing everyone's attention to her.

Gabe held Shantae's eyes once more.

"Who's supposedly the new team that's pushing coke lower than the price I'm sure you and the rest of y'all know Brianna's people are pushing theirs for?"

"I'm not exactly sure who's behind the coke, but I know a lieutenant who's over at a spot out in Overtown," Shantae explained to him.

"What's dude's name, Shan?"

Shantae was caught off guard and surprised to hear Gabe use the nickname that he gave her when they once dated. She got control of herself and responded.

"His name's Show Time!"

"Show Time, huh?" Gabe repeated, smiling at

her.

He then looked over to Silk, out of respect, wanting to keep the peace.

"You mind if Shantae rolls with me real quick?"

Silk laughed lightly and smiled a bit at the question that Gabe had just asked him.

"She's her own woman, Gabe. And besides, homeboy, Shantae's not my woman!"

Gabe was surprised at the confession, and he looked back at Shantae and met up with her eyes again.

"So, what's up, ma? You feel like showing me where this fool-ass dude is at?"

"How about we all go?" Duke said, drawing everyone's attention to him, except Gabe's and Shantae's.

"What you planning, fam?" Gabe asked him while still holding Shantae's gaze.

"My G! You already know what the plan is!" Duke said with a smile as he stared around at the rest of the team before looking back at Gabe, who was finally looking at him.

"We were already planning on getting at this same clown. Dude has a team, but shit's weak out there!"

Gabe slowly nodded his head after listening to Duke, and then noticed both Silk and Boo Man watching and waiting on him. He then looked back at Shantae.

"You still carry two bangers on you?"

"Of course!" Shantae answered as she lifted her pants leg and pulled a chrome .40 caliber from its ankle holster.

She walked over to stand in front of Gabe and handed him the piece's handle first.

After taking the .40 and not bothering to check the magazine, since he knew how Shantae got down, Gabe stood up from his spot on the sofa and slid the hammer into his jeans at the small of his back.

"Y'all, let's get this over with!"

"That's what the fuck I'm talking about!" Duke said, hyped up to have his ace back with him.

CHAPTER 3

A fter leaving Duke and Melody's apartment, Shantae rode shotgun alone with Gabe while Duke, Silk, and Boo Man trailed behind in a Cadillac Escalade Gabe found out belonged to Silk. Gabe followed Shantae's directions, but neither of them said much of anything else to the other in the car.

"Gabe!" Shantae spoke up, breaking the silence between the two of them and looking over at him. "We need to talk. I need to get this out!"

"Shantae, we don't need—!"

"Gabe, I still love you!" Shantae admitted, cutting him off and seeing the change in his facial expression. She continued once he remained quiet. "I should have explained this to you when we were still together, but I was young and didn't know anything about having a real boyfriend. I knew Silk was in love with me, and I knew he hated that I fell in love with you and not him. But I never said anything to him because I didn't want to hurt him. Gabe, he's my best friend, and I didn't—!"

"I was supposed to be your best friend, Shantae!" Gabe spoke up, interrupting her again. "I was the one that fell in love with you and would do whatever for you, but you chose him over us!"

"That's the problem right there!" she told him. "I never chose Silk over us. I only wanted to be with you, but I didn't know how to tell Silk so I wouldn't hurt him. But in the end, I was the one that was hurt, because I hurt the one person I fell in love with and still love. And that's you, Gabe!"

Gabe slowly shook his head as he glanced back over at Shantae and gave a little laugh under his breath.

"Why are you telling me this now, Shan?"

"Because I want my man back!" she replied. While staring straight at him, she reached over and grabbed the side of his face. "I want us back together, Gabe. I miss and love you!"

"Shan, that's not—!"

"Don't say nothing!" she told him, cutting Gabe off. "Just let me prove myself to you! I'll prove how much I love you and want us to be together."

Gabe cut his eyes over toward Shantae and saw the seriousness and sincerity in them and heard it in her voice. He gave her a simple nod of the head and said nothing else in response to what she had just told him.

~ ~ ~

Once they arrived in Overtown, they all followed Shantae's directions to the block where the trap spot was that was run by Show Time. They could also see the flow of customers. Gabe peeped the Escalade stopping at the corner. He didn't care about the Lexus being seen, since he had already planned to deal with Show Time, being that this was his second time dealing with the clown.

He parked the Lexus right across the street from the apartment and climbed out, with Shantae following behind him. Gabe started across the street using his eyes and looking around the area. He saw two lookouts on the corners on the opposite end, and four workers out in front of the apartment making sales.

Gabe locked in on the biggest of the four guys. He ignored the buyers and walked straight up to the stocky man.

"What up, my nigga?" the big man asked, looking Gabe up and down. "What you looking for?"

"I'm looking for Show Time!" Gabe replied, noticing the other three workers all looking his way after hearing their boss's name. "Go get him and bring him to me, or do I have to go inside and get 'im myself?"

"What?" the big man said and then began laughing. He then looked to his right. "Y'all hear this?"

Never giving homeboy a chance to finish what he was saying, Gabe punched the big man straight to the throat, causing him to choke on his own words. Gabe then stepped into a little leap, spinning into a round-house kick that connected with the side of the man's face and sent his big ass straight to the ground hard, knocking him out.

Gabe stood over the big man and stared down at his sleeping body. He then looked over at the dark-skinned guy beside him who stood, like everybody else, with a shocked expression on his face.

"Same question I asked the big dummy!" Gabe told the guy. "What's your answer?"

"I got ya, my nigga!" the guy stated as he rushed off, jumping over his still sleeping homeboy.

"Good decision!" Gabe replied as he turned back to face Shantae.

She was just staring at him with a look of

disbelief, but still holding her Glock .40 gripped inside her right hand against her thigh.

"What the fuck was that shit?" she questioned Gabe as she then walked over to stand beside him.

"What was what?" he asked as he peeped Duke, Silk, and Boo Man creeping up the side of the apartment.

"Nigga, don't play with me!" Shantae responded, just as she heard the banging of a front door.

She then saw the blur of movement beside her, and just as she was turning to see what Gabe was doing, she jumped in surprise at the sound of a gun going off.

Boom! Boom! Boom!

"What the fuck!" Shantae heard, seeing her brother, Silk, and Boo Man rushing up from the side of the apartment. She then looked at Gabe as he walked off.

Shantae finally heard the screaming that was around her, and she saw two guys on the ground. One of them was the dark-skinned guy who Gabe had sent into the apartment. He was now laid out on the ground with an AK-47 beside him and a bullet hole to his face. The other man, a light, brown-skinned man, lay on the ground bleeding badly from both knees and screaming in pain.

"What the hell?" Shantae said to herself as she walked up beside Gabe, who was now squatted down beside the man with the blown-out knees.

She could hear Gabe asking him questions after slapping him across the face when he would not stop yelling and crying.

"Bruh, let's bounce!" Duke said as he, Boo Man, and Silk rushed out of the apartment with three bags.

"I'ma a catch up with y'all," Gabe told Duke. "I'll hit you up after I leave here!"

"Fam, you sure about that?" Boo Man asked, not really feeling the whole idea of leaving Gabe behind.

"I'ma get up later, Big Homie!" Gabe told Boo Man, and then winked at him with a smirk on his face.

"I'm staying with Gabe!" Shantae told her brother and the others.

"Naw!" Gabe answered, looking up at Shantae. "Go ahead with Duke and them."

"Excuse me?"

"Shan, just do as I ask you."

"Hell no!" she went off. "I'm not leaving you

here by yourself."

"Shantae, just do as I ask, ma," Gabe told her as he stood back up to his feet and faced her. He lowered his voice to a whisper. "Shan, I got everything under control. I need you to trust me and let me talk to you later."

Shantae hated to leave, but she wanted to show him how serious she was about him. So, she dug out her cell phone and placed it into his free left hand. She then surprised him as she stepped into him and kissed him directly on the lips.

"You better answer the phone when I call you in one hour!" she told him before taking off and catching up with her brother and the others.

Gabe shook his head as he watched Shantae run off. He then looked back at Show Time, who was sweating and breathing fast.

"Now, where was we?" Gabe asked as he squatted back down beside the dumb-ass supposed hustler. "Who's your boss?"

~ ~ ~

Brianna looked at the wall clock again for the fifth or however many times she already looked, and saw that it was 3:30 p.m. Gabe had still not shown up, and Lorenzo had also still not called her after she sent him to find Gabe. She snatched up the cell phone from the glass coffee table as soon as it started to ring.

"Gabe?"

"This Lorenzo."

"You found Gabe? Where was he?"

"I ain't find 'im, Brianna, but I'm pretty sure I know where the boy been at though!"

"Wait!" Brianna said, confused. "What do you mean you think you know where Gabe's been?"

She listened to Lorenzo as he told her about the double murder that he heard about and was now in Overtown watching as the police asked questions but got even fewer answers. They were only informed of a few stories of men dressed in all black and wearing ski masks. Brianna stopped listening when she heard Duchess begin barking, so she was about to get up and go to the front door.

"Lorenzo, hold on!" she told him as she got up from the sofa.

But as soon as she walked out of the den, the front door opened and Gabe walked into the penthouse.

Brianna informed Lorenzo that Gabe was home

and that she would call him back later. She then hung up the phone and simply stared at her man petting the dog's head with a big smile on his face.

"Hey!" Gabe said as he stood up and started toward her.

"Hey, you!" she replied back as she kissed her man's lips and deeply sighed as she hugged him.

They both walked into the den, and Brianna sat down on the sofa. Duchess hopped up and lay beside Gabe. Brianna shook her head, not even bothering to tell the dog to get down. Instead, she asked where he had been.

"Visiting Show Time!" Gabe answered as he pulled out the black touch-screen he took from him after putting a bullet into his head.

He handed the phone to Brianna and said, "The name of the guy who was supplying Show Time is in the phone."

"What's the name?" she asked as she pulled up the directory on the phone.

"It's Peter Snow!"

Brianna found the name and started to call him. But then she looked over at Gabe and asked, "You've called already, haven't you?"

Gabe nodded his head and then explained that he wanted her to keep bodyguards around her at all times whenever he wasn't around and until he said differently.

"What are you planning, Gabe?" she asked him as she set down the touch-screen.

"If things go as I'm planning, this Peter Snow guy is going to show himself because after losing five bricks of cocaine and a little over $70,000 in cash, I'm pretty sure he's gonna want both and his respect back since I made it known that I work for you now!"

"So, basically, you've made me a target is what you're saying, isn't it? she asked, with a growing attitude.

"That's exactly why when I'm not with you and you leave this penthouse, you're gonna have a team of bodyguards with you!" Gabe told her.

Brianna was just about to open her mouth.

"Also, I fired those clowns that were supposed to be watching your back in the Range Rover. So you can do things my way or let your Darrell stick you with a team of escorts, whichever you wanna choose!"

Brianna sucked her teeth and then playfully punched him in the arm.

"You make me sick, boy!"

"Yeah, I love you too!" Gabe said as he pulled Brianna over into his lap and passionately kissed her lips.

Brianna moaned as she felt both of Gabe's hands grip her butt. She then broke the kiss and tried to catch her breath.

"Let's go to the bedroom!"

"I was thinking the same exact thing!" he said as he easily picked her up, causing her to scream and giggle as he walked her from the den to the other side of the penthouse and into their bedroom.

He gently laid her down on the bed and smiled as Brianna quickly began snatching off her own clothes.

"You in a hurry, huh?" Gabe asked playfully as he smiled while also beginning to get undressed.

"Boy, it's been over a year!" Brianna reminded him, tossing her bra and then her panties to the floor. "I'm tired of waiting. Now if you don't get in this bed, I'm going to take what I want, understand!"

Gabe laughed and then climbed into the bed and in between her thick thighs as she reached up for him.

CHAPTER 4

Gabe lay in bed next to his fiancée but was unable to sleep, even after almost two hours of sex with Brianna. She had tapped out when she finally had enough. Instead, he lay staring up at the ceiling and thinking about somebody else while his woman was in the bed with him. He sighed softly and deeply as he climbed out of bed and heard Brianna moan softly but remain asleep.

Gabe grabbed his jeans and pulled them, and then heard Duchess crying lightly. He called to her and watched as Duchess hopped up from her bed in the bedroom and followed him as he walked out of the bedroom door. He shut the door behind him and Duchess, and the two of them walked to the kitchen. Gabe grabbed a bottle of apple juice for himself and a handful of Milk Bones for the dog.

He walked out onto the terrace, shutting the glass door behind them. He sat down on the small couch in the dimly lit corner facing the sliding glass door. Duchess immediately jumped up into his lap.

After feeding the dog some Milk Bones, he set the rest of them in front of her on his lap while he opened his juice and took a sip.

"Finished already, huh?" Gabe said once he lowered the juice bottle to see Duchess watching him. "You getting too big, you know that?"

Gabe smiled as Duchess jumped from his lap over to drink water out of a bowl on the terrace. He brushed off his jeans and then picked up the phone that Shantae had given him and saw eleven missed calls, all from a number that had Shantae's name attached to it.

He called the number and heard the line ring.

"Gabe?" a voice said at the start of the second ring.

"Yeah, Shan!"

Gabe heard her sigh loudly, and he asked, "You still up?"

"I was just about to call the phone again!" she admitted, but then said, "I won't ask why you didn't answer, but I did see the news!"

"I did too!"

Both remained quiet for a few brief moments, when Shantae broke the silence. "Did you think about what I said, Gabe?"

"Yeah, Shan!" he answered. "But it's too late for

all that. I'm with Brianna."

"So, you don't love me anymore? Is that what you're saying?"

"Shantae, let's not—!"

"Answer the question, Gabe!"

"For what? What is it gonna prove?"

"It'll prove that I'm still the one you want, just like you're the one I want and need, Gabe! I love you!"

"I hear you, Shantae!"

"I know you do! But do you still love me like ya said you once did?"

Gabe sighed as he stood up and walked over to the rail. He leaned against it as he held the phone up against his ear.

"Shan, I really don't see what the point of this conversation is. You know I'm with Brianna, and I'm sure you're kicking it with somebody else right now anyway."

"You're wrong!" Shantae told him. "And even if I was seeing someone, you're number one in my life, Gabe! I would leave whoever for you!"

"Shantae!"

"Gabe, I wanna see you," she told him,

interrupting what Gabe was about to say. "Can I see you?"

"Shan, it's almost—!"

"Can I see you or not, Gabe?"

Gabe sighed loudly. He knew what he was considering was wrong, but he heard himself asking where Shantae wanted to meet up.

~ ~ ~

Shantae waited inside the den at her condo after hanging up with Gabe once he finally agreed to come over and see her. She was nervous but was trying to stay calm by smoking a blunt that was flavored with bubble gum. She paid little attention to the movie that was playing on the flat-screen.

She turned her head and looked at the window when she heard his car pull up. She saw the headlights shining through her windows, so she set the blunt inside the glass ashtray and then stood to her feet and started toward the front door.

She unlocked the door and saw Gabe's Escalade EXT truck. She stood at her door waiting for him to get out. She couldn't see too much inside of his truck because of the tinted windows. She got tired of waiting, so she stepped out onto her porch and then walked down to his truck to the driver's door.

"Come on!" she told Gabe after opening the driver's door and reaching inside and taking his hand.

Once she got Gabe out of the truck, she led him into her condo and then shut and locked the door behind her. She then headed into her den, still leading Gabe by the hand.

"Sit down!" Shantae told him after sitting back down on her sofa and watching Gabe as he sighed and took a seat beside her.

"Shan, I shouldn't be here!" he finally spoke up.

"Yes, you should!" she told him while staring at him.

She was half facing him with her left leg folded underneath her.

"You can keep telling yourself differently Gabe, but you and I both know this is where you belong."

Gabe shook his head and started to get back up, just as Shantae leaned over and kissed him.

They were both unsure exactly how it happened, but they were lying together across the sofa with Shantae on top of Gabe and passionately kissing him. Shantae then broke the kiss after a moment and looked into Gabe's eyes.

"I love you, Gabe."

"Shan, I love you too!" Gabe admitted. "But I'm with Brianna!"

"Do you love her?"

"Yeah, I do, Shan!"

"But do you want to be with me or her, Gabe?" Shantae asked him as she ran her hand through the thick hair on his head that was surprisingly soft and just slightly beginning to turn wavy.

Gabe wrapped his arms around her as he turned onto his side and placed her on the sofa in front of him. He rested his face in her silky, raven-black, shoulder-length hair as she laid her head on his chest. She wrapped her right arm around him and remained quiet since he was unable to answer her question.

"I love you too, Gabe!" Shantae told him, speaking into his chest.

~ ~ ~

"Shan!"

She felt someone gently shaking her awake while hearing her name being called. She opened her eyes and smiled when she looked up and met Gabe's eyes.

"Hi!" she replied as she leaned forward and

36

kissed Gabe on the lips. "What time is it anyway?"

"It's six twenty in the morning," Gabe informed her as he brushed back some hair out of Shantae's face.

He then bent down and kissed her forehead and then said, "I need to get going, ma!"

"I know," Shantae said, sighing as she slowly sat up from beside him. She looked back over to him as he was also sitting up. "What are we going to do, Gabe?"

Gabe looked back over at Shantae after hearing her question.

"I honestly don't know, Shan. I really don't know, ma!"

She leaned over and wrapped her arms around his neck. She hugged him and then kissed his cheek.

"I won't keep pushing you, Gabe! Just know that I love you and I want us to get back together."

"I know, Shan!" Gabe stated, leaning over and kissing her again before the two of them stood up and started toward the front door.

Once Gabe was outside and walking to his truck with Shantae, he hit the locks and opened the truck. He remembered that he still had her phone, so he dug it from his pocket and handed it back to her.

"I'ma grab a cell phone today," Gabe told her. "So look for the text with the new number in it."

She smiled as she stood watching him climb into his truck. She waited until he had the Escalade started and was backing out from in front of her condo. She then turned and started back toward her front door.

Gabe watched as Shantae walked back inside. He drove off after she shut the front door, and he then started back across town. As he was driving, different thoughts ran through his mind. He was not surprised that he still had feelings for Shantae, but he was shocked at how strong they were, even after all the time that had passed and they had not seen each other.

Gabe was unsure exactly how to handle the new problem of dealing with Shantae and her wanting them back together while he was still with Brianna. Not to mention that he was still engaged to her and was employed by her family. He reached their apartment building a little while later and parked inside the garage between the 1975 Buick LeSabre and his 1974 Chevy Caprice.

He exited the garage and took the elevator up to

their floor. He then stepped off and walked down the hall toward their front door. He used his key to unlock the door and stepped inside, only to find Duchess waiting at the door.

"Hey, girl!" Gabe said as he shut and locked the door behind him.

He bent down and rubbed Duchess under her neck before he headed to the other side of the penthouse. He walked into the master bedroom to find Brianna still asleep and curled up with his pillow.

Gabe stood at the side of the bed and just watched Brianna as she slept a few moments. He sighed as he began undressing and then climbed into bed.

"Where'd you go?" Brianna asked in a half-asleep voice as she slid over to lie under Gabe, wrapping her arms across his middle.

Gabe heard the deep breathing before he attempted to answer her, realizing that she had already fallen back asleep. He wrapped his arm around her and sighed tiredly as he too closed his eyes to try to get back to sleep.

CHAPTER 5

Brianna was awakened by the sound of her ringing cell phone. She groaned and rolled over to her left, picking it up from the nightstand.

"Hello!" Brianna said into the phone, rolling back onto her side.

"I see there's a different attitude this morning. How are you now that Gabriel has returned home?"

Brianna recognized her step-father's voice seconds after she realized that Gabe wasn't asleep and in bed next to her. She told her step-father that she would call him right back as she was climbing out of bed. She quickly slipped into a pair of gray cotton sweatpants and then headed out of the bedroom to look around for Gabe.

"What in the hell?" Brianna cried out in shock and disbelief as she stood in the entranceway to the den.

She stared at Gabe and all the stacks and stacks of money that were all over the coffee table. She then noticed even more inside a black leather duffel bag that was on the floor beside Gabe's left leg.

"Bri, what's up?" Gabe said after noticing her in

the entranceway.

"Gabe, where the hell did all this money come from, boy?" Brianna asked as she walked over to sit on the couch to the left of him, staring at all the money that was laid out before her.

"It's the money that Paul Lewis owed before I left for training."

"Who?"

"The $75 million, Brianna!" Gabe reminded her.

After remembering, Brianna could still only stare at the money.

"That's $75 million?" she asked.

"Naw! That's $25 million you're looking at," Gabe answered, just as his new Samsung Galaxy S9 began ringing beside him on the sofa.

After picking it up, Gabe answered without checking to see who was calling: "Yeah!"

He listened to Duke announce that he and Boo Man were downstairs. Gabe told his boy that he was on his way down in a few minutes and then hung up the phone.

"Gabe, where are you going?" Brianna asked as soon as he hung up the phone. "And whose phone is that you're using?"

"I gotta handle something with Duke and them!" he told her as he was packing up the money from the coffee table into the backpack that was setting on his right on the sofa. He got up from the sofa and added, "I also programmed my number into your phone, and I've already assigned a team to watch you. But they won't interfere unless something happens, and don't be trying to lose ya team, Brianna!"

"Gabe, where are you going?" Brianna asked again as she quickly followed him to the front door.

"I just wanna handle something real quick," he told her, just as the knocking started at the door.

He opened it and saw Sherry and Tamara standing there. Gabe received a kiss to the cheek from both women as he walked out the door.

"Where's he going?" Sherry asked as she walked inside.

"I don't even know, girl!" Brianna answered, looking out into the hall just in time to see Gabe step into the elevator.

Brianna shut and locked the door and then joined Tamara and Sherry inside the kitchen as they all gave their breakfast orders to the butler, Eddie.

~ ~ ~

"Hey, Shantae, girl!" Melody said, surprised to open her front door and find her soon-to-be sister-in-law standing there. "What are you doing here?"

"Melody, we need to talk!" Shantae began while walking into the apartment.

After closing and locking the door behind Shantae, Melody turned around to find Shantae walking backward and forward nervously.

"Girl, what's wrong with you?"

"Melody, it's Gabe! I really need to talk to you!" she explained as Melody grabbed her hand and led her over into the den.

"Alright! What's wrong with Gabe?" Melody asked Shantae once the two of them were seated inside the den. "Tell me what happened!"

Shantae sighed loudly and deeply and then confessed to talking with Gabe the night before on the phone.

"There's nothing wrong with that, Shantae!" Melody told her. "What's wrong with the two of you being friends and talking?"

"That's just it, Melody!" Shantae stated in a tone that made Melody sit up straighter. "Gabe came to my place last night and we slept together."

"Oh my God!" Melody cried. "Shantae, are you serious? Did you really have sex with Gabe?"

"What?" Shantae said, staring at Melody with a confused look. "Melody, what the hell you talking about?"

"You just said you and Gabe slept together!"

"We did!"

"Wait!" Melody said, holding up her hand for Shantae to keep quiet. After getting her thoughts together for a moment, she continued, "Shantae, you telling me you and Gabe actually just slept together as in sleeping, right?"

"That's what I said!" Shantae reiterated to Melody. "Ain't nobody say nothing about fucking Gabe!"

Melody waved her hand at Shantae and said, "Just finish explaining what you was saying, Shantae."

Doing as Melody requested, Shantae finished her story and explained about the talk she and Gabe had last night with him confessing that he still loved her, but that he also loved Brianna.

"So what are you gonna do, Shantae?" Melody asked her. "You knew before you and Gabe decided to spend the night together and start telling each other your feelings, that he was still with that Brianna girl!"

"That's just it, Melody!" Shantae started. "I don't care who Gabe is with. He belongs with me! I love him, Melody, and I will kill that bitch Brianna and whoever else stands in my way of being with him!"

Melody was in complete and utter shock and surprise at what she was seeing at that very moment. She stared open-mouthed and watched as Shantae actually cried, with tears running down her face.

"Come here, girl!" Melody said, pulling her friend over into a hug, holding the normally tough and read-to-beat-a-bitch-up type of female. "I don't know how we gonna do this, but we will find a way to get the two of you together. I just have one question, Shantae."

"What?" she asked as she pulled back to meet Melody's eyes.

"What about this guy Tyree you been seeing?" Melody questioned. "Does Gabe know about him, and what are you gonna do since you already know how Tyree feels about you?"

Shantae was unable to really answer Melody's

question, since she, in fact, knew how Tyree could get about her. But she also knew how Gabe could get, which was twenty times worse than Tyree. Shantae groaned as she ran both hands through her hair. She was unsure exactly how she was going to deal with what she was in the middle of.

~ ~ ~

Brianna climbed from the Benz truck that she parked at the front of her mother and step-father's estate, with Tamara and Sherry in tow. Brianna spotted her step-sister Erica's new BMW X1 truck that she had just bought and then shook her head. She wasn't really in the right space to deal with Erica at the moment.

"Brianna, what's up with Gabe?" Sherry asked her. "Did you get in contact with my boo, Bri?"

"I texted his ass!" Brianna informed her as she was putting away her phone. "But his ass acts like he's too busy to contact me back! Wait til I see him!"

Brianna chatted with her mother and Darrell's butler, who held open the door for the girls as the three of them entered. Brianna found out from him where her mother and Darrell were in the house.

The three of them stepped into the kitchen, and

Brianna gave her mother, Victoria Murphy, a hug. After Victoria broke the embrace, she wanted to know where Gabe was.

"Maybe you should call his ass since he won't answer my calls!" Brianna told her mother, catching a quick attitude as she turned and left the kitchen.

Brianna then made her way to Darrell's office and knocked on the door, but she entered before she was invited inside. She instantly spotted a tall, brown-skinned, Hulk-like-built guy standing beside her step-sister, Erica, who was sitting on one of the two couches in Darrell's office.

"Where's Gabriel, Brianna?" Darrell asked, expecting his daughter's fiancé to walk in behind her.

"I have no idea!" Brianna told her step-father. "But if you find him, please let me know because I haven't seen him since he left the apartment this morning!"

"I bet you know where to find Anthony though!" Erica mumbled loud enough that Brianna heard her.

"Excuse me?" Brianna said, turning to face Erica. "What the hell you just say?"

Erica waved her hand dismissively at Brianna, all the while smiling.

"Daddy, can we get this over with? I've got other things I really need to do as well!" Erica said, looking at her father.

"I bet you do!" Brianna stated, rolling her eyes. "Nasty bitch!"

"Excuse you!" Erica responded with a balled-up face.

"Bitch! You heard me!" Brianna said as she started toward Erica, only to be cut off as the big man in the dark blue suit stepped in front of her. She looked the guy over and then nastily said, "Who the hell is you? You need to get out my way before something bad happens to your big stupid ass!"

"Enough!" Darrell yelled before calling to Brianna after being ignored.

"She gives warnings, but I don't!" a voice announced.

Everyone in the room heard and recognized a new voice and then looked toward the door. Brianna began to smile after seeing her baby. She watched as Gabe walked over and positioned himself in front of her while facing the big man in the suit.

"Gabe!" Erica cried out, smiling as she quickly grabbed the big man and pulled him back away from

Gabe. "Oh my God! You really are home, and you look good!"

"What's up, Erica?" Gabe stated, but never took his eyes off the big man.

"Gabriel," Darrell called out to him, trying to stop anything from happening, since he knew from the reports he got back that his soon-to-be son-in-law was not the same young man he was before he left.

Gabe heard Darrell, but he did not respond. He turned his back on the big man and faced Brianna. "You alright, ma?"

She nodded her head and smiled at the sight of her man in the black metallic jeans he was wearing along with a long-sleeved Polo pullover sweater, brown-and-cream-colored shirt, and brown Tims on his feet. She accepted the kiss he gave her and sighed as she wrapped her arms around his waist.

"Sorry I'm late!" Gabe began, directing his attention to Darrell now. "There were a few things I had to handle, but what's up?"

Darrell nodded his head in understanding and smiled at the sight of his future son-in-law. Darrell then asked everyone to take a seat, and then he introduced everyone to Frank, Erica's new bodyguard.

"What the hell does she need a bodyguard for?" Brianna questioned, shooting a look over at her step-sister.

"I'm going to explain that now, Brianna!" Darrell told her as he shook his head. "Frank is going to be Erica's bodyguard now that she's decided to join the family business. She will also join the operation I've set up with you, Brianna."

"What?" Brianna yelled as she shot up out of her seat.

She stared at her step-father as if he was insane, only for Gabe to gently grab her hand to get her attention.

"Bri, just hear him out!" Gabe suggested while gently pulling Brianna back down onto the couch beside him.

Darrell allowed a small smile to show as he nodded his head in thanks to Gabe. He then sat back inside his tall black leather desk chair. He folded his hands on his lap and continued what he was trying to explain.

~ ~ ~

Brianna walked straight out of her step-father's

office as soon as the meeting was over. She then headed toward the front of the mansion, ignoring Gabe, who was calling her from behind. She made it to the front door just as she heard Erica call out to Gabe.

Brianna turned around to see Erica walk up to Gabe, wrap her arms around his neck, and press her body against him. Brianna didn't even realize she was moving until she was already up on Erica and grabbing her by the hair.

"Ahhhhh!" Erica screamed as Brianna jerked her head backward.

"Bitch! I told you—!" Brianna started.

But she stopped in the middle of what she was saying when she felt strong hands grip her around the back of the neck for a brief moment. However, she felt the hands release her even quicker and then heard the sound of something heavy hitting the ground behind her.

Brianna spun around to see Erica's bodyguard lying facedown on the floor with Gabe, holding Frank's left arm behind his back and a Glock .50 pressed against the back of his head.

"What's going on out here?" Darrell yelled as he

walked out to the front of the mansion at the same time that Victoria was coming down the front stairs. "Gabriel, what's going on?"

"It's nothing, daddy!" Erica quickly spoke up, pulling Gabe off of Frank and meeting his eyes a brief moment before Brianna grabbed his arm and began leading him away.

Once they were outside, Brianna was caught off guard when she saw Sherry, Tamara, and Lorenzo talking with Gabe's friends, Duke and Boo Man. But she paused right where she was when her eyes landed on Gabe's ex-girlfriend leaning against a stratus-gray metallic Porsche 911 45 Targa.

"What the fuck is that bitch doing here, Gabe?" Brianna asked while now locking eyes with Gabe's ex-bitch.

Gabe heard Brianna, but he didn't bother answering her since he saw that she was in one of her moods after the meeting and what had just happened with Erica and Frank. Gabe dug out his keys and tossed them over to Shantae.

"Follow us!" he told Shantae before he turned back to Brianna and met but ignored the look on her face. "Gimme ya keys!"

"Hell no, nigga!" Brianna told Gabe just as Duke called out to him.

"Get in the truck, Brianna!" Gabe ordered before walking over to Duke as he stood with Boo Man and Brianna's team next to Duke's Range Rover Supercharged.

Brianna sucked her teeth as she rolled her eyes at Gabe, even as his ass walked off. She called to Sherry and Tamara and told them they were leaving as she walked around to the driver's side of her Benz truck.

"Yo, Brianna!" Lorenzo called as he opened the front passenger door.

"What, Lorenzo?" she replied. "You coming with us or what?"

"You do hear Gabe calling you, right?" Lorenzo asked as he stood in front of the open passenger door.

"Are you coming with us or not?" Brianna asked him again as she started up the truck.

Lorenzo glanced over at Gabe and saw the boy watching Brianna but also talking to someone on his cell phone. Lorenzo gave Gabe a nod before climbing into the truck beside Brianna.

~ ~ ~

Gabe watched Brianna drive off while listening

to Duke's friend to whom he was introduced. The friend was supposed to find out any information he could on whoever Peter Snow was and where to find him.

"Your boys ready to work?" Gabe asked, tossing Duke back his phone.

"We're already on it!" Duke replied to him, catching the phone as he and Boo Man jogged off.

Gabe watched as both his boys hopped into Duke's new truck. He then turned back to the Porsche to see Shantae off away talking in a lowered voice on her cell phone, but he noticed the look on her face.

"Shan, let's go. Time to get outta here!" Gabe called as he climbed into the car from the passenger side.

"Where we going?" Shantae asked once she finally got into the car.

"You remember where my pops and step-mom's house is?" he asked her.

"Of course!" she answered. "We going there?"

"Yeah!" Gabe replied as Shantae pulled off from the estate.

Gabe picked up the soft pack of Newports from

the center console and took out a cigarette. He then asked Shantae if she was okay.

"Why wouldn't I be?" Shantae asked, glancing over at Gabe.

"Who was that on the phone?" he asked.

She remained quiet a brief moment and looked back at Gabe, who sat smoking a cigarette and staring out the window.

"It was nothing, Gabe. I can handle it!" she simply said.

"Yeah!" was all that Gabe said back.

~ ~ ~

They made it out to Gabe's father and step-mother's house to see an extremely excited Nicole. She screamed once she opened the front door, and jumped into Gabe's arms after realizing who he was. Gabe paid no attention to his father or step-brothers once he walked into the house, but he noticed the way the three of them all stared openly at him.

He decided to treat Nicole to dinner at the new seafood restaurant she mentioned that she liked, which was now her favorite restaurant. However, Nicole apologized and asked if they could reschedule after she told him that she could not go since she and his father were about to go out on a business lunch date. But Gabe got her to agree to lunch the next day.

"Let me use the bathroom and then we're leaving, Shan," Gabe told her, leaving her and Nicole on the front porch while he walked back into the house.

After the front door closed behind him, Nicole wasted no time questioning Shantae.

"So, how long have you two been seeing each other, Shantae?"

"Umm, excuse me?" she asked, caught completely off guard by the question. "What are you talking about?"

"Shantae, sweetie, I'm not blind, and yes, I remember you!" Nicole told her. "You came here looking for Gabriel some time back before he left town on the business trip he went on. I remember how hurt and disappointed you looked when I told you he was with his girlfriend, but now I see a totally different attitude, not just with you, but also with Gabriel. When did he call off his engagement, and when did you two begin seeing each other?"

Shantae was surprised at what she had just heard the woman break down to her. She sighed as she ran her hand through her hair before she admitted the truth.

"Mrs. Green, Gabe and I aren't seeing each other, and he hasn't called off his engagement. He's still engaged to Brianna."

"Does she know that you're in love with Gabe?"

Nicole noticed the surprised look that strengthened itself after the question she asked Shantae.

"Sweetheart, don't look so surprised that I knew. It's shown all over your face whenever you look at my step-son or even whenever Gabriel simply stands next to you. I'll tell you another thing too!" she began with a smile.

"Shan, you ready?" Gabe asked as he walked out of the house unknowingly interrupting their conversation. He kissed Nicole on the cheek and hugged her tightly. "I'ma see you tomorrow."

"Okay, sweetheart!" Nicole replied, smiling at him before she then called to Shantae and asked if she could speak to her a moment before she left.

"Yeah!" Shantae said as she switched her attention from Gabe walking out to the Porsche, back to Nicole. "What's up?"

"I just wanted to tell you that if what you feel for Gabriel is truly how you feel, then I approve. My only advice is that you don't hurt him, and always make sure he's able to trust you, Shantae. He's been through a lot, and trust is a very major issue with him. I even had to earn it. Just be careful, sweetie!"

Shantae was surprised, but was very accepting of the hug that Gabe's step-mother suddenly gave her. Shantae returned the hug as they said their goodbyes.

Once she made her way to the Porsche and climbed behind the wheel, she noticed the way Gabe was watching her.

"So, where are we going now?" she asked as she started the engine while ignoring Gabe's gaze.

~ ~ ~

Brianna made her way through the city after visiting a few other spots that she and her team ran. She pulled up in front of the spot that Jit Jit ran, and was very happy to see that business was back up and running. She parked in the street in front of the spot and saw Jit Jit walking out to her truck when he noticed her Benz pull up.

"What's up, y'all?" Jit Jit said after the passenger window came down and he first saw Lorenzo. He then peeped both Sherry and Tamara in the back seat.

"Business is looking back to normal!" Brianna stated, looking past Jit Jit to see the flow of customers and even a few rides pulling up to also buy. "How's everything else though?"

"Y'all just missed out on the bullshit a few minutes before you pulled up!" he informed Brianna and the others. He told them about another visit, by two boys who worked for Peter Snow.

"What they talking about?" Lorenzo asked him.

"They wanna know who the crew was that Brianna sent out to Overtown that bodied two of his men," Jit Jit explained.

"How the hell he knows it's me?" Brianna asked. "Ain't nobody knows nothing about Gabe and his friends, Jit Jit!"

"Think about it, Brianna," Jit Jit began. "After the bullshit that just happened and the threat that you just got, who else could have made the move if not us?"

"But ain't none of us knows who was behind the threat!" Sherry said as she sat forward between the two front seats to see Jit Jit.

Brianna heard the engine and looked out her

window to see the same Porsche from her step-father and mother's mansion. She sat watching as the Porsche stopped beside her, and Gabe climbed out of the passenger seat.

"Speak of my dude!" Lorenzo stated, smiling at seeing Gabe.

"What up, y'all?" Gabe said as he approached the driver's window and nodded across to Lorenzo.

He then leaned in through the driver's window to kiss Brianna, only to have her push him back away from her.

"Just who the hell is that driving you around, Gabe?" Brianna asked him with a growing attitude.

"It's Shantae!" he answered truthfully just as Duke's Range Rover pulled up behind Brianna's truck.

Gabe then turned his attention back to Brianna, only to see her staring past him. He looked back over his right shoulder to see Shantae climbing out of the Porsche and heading over to Duke's Range Rover. He looked back at Brianna as she went off.

"Why the fuck is you still with that bitch, Gabe?" Brianna yelled. "I already told you that I don't want your ass with or around that bitch, and yet you just continue to do what the hell you want!"

Gabe heard Brianna but then peeped the dark blue Navigator when it slowly turned down the street and began creeping in their direction. Gabe was already pulling out his Glock .50 just as Lorenzo was hopping out of the truck the same time the Navigator hit the gas and took off up the street.

"Shan, it's a drive-by!" Gabe yelled at the same time both he and Lorenzo started letting off rounds.

Boom! Boom! Boom! Boom! Boom! Boom! Boom!

Shantae heard Gabe's warning seconds before the shooting started. She ducked down and pulled out her own Glock as she saw the Navigator go flying past, only to see Gabe and Lorenzo take off behind the SUV on foot.

She then took off toward the Porsche and hopped behind the wheel. Within moments, she had the Porsche shooting up the street behind Gabe and Lorenzo. Hearing the horn being blown from behind them, both Gabe and Lorenzo looked back to see the new Porsche that Gabe just bought pulling up to them.

"Get the fuck in!" Shantae told them both.

Gabe allowed Lorenzo inside, but he crazily sat on the window sill on the passenger side of the Porsche.

Shantae pushed the new Porsche to its maximum speed, but she was still worried even though Lorenzo was holding onto Gabe's legs to keep him from falling out the window. She noticed that the Navigator was getting in view as they got closer. After a few more minutes, she heard Gabe call to Lorenzo to pass up his gun.

"Shan, get closer!" Gabe yelled into the car.

Shantae did as she was told and got the Porsche closer. Right after the first shot was fired, the back window of the Navigator exploded. She heard two more shots, and the back two tires blew out, causing the SUV to lose control and begin flipping. She had to slam on the brakes and snatch the wheel a hard right to miss hitting the SUV herself.

"Gabe, what the fuck!" Shantae yelled after his crazy ass hopped out of the window, only to be followed by Lorenzo, who actually had a smile on his face.

"What in the hell is wrong with them?" Shantae said out loud to herself.

She then watched Lorenzo and Gabe walk over to the Navigator while the sounds of police cars were getting closer.

Gabe looked inside the flipped SUV and saw that the three men in the back seat were all dead, but the man in the passenger seat was still breathing but was fucked up bad. Gabe and Lorenzo were pulling the passenger out of the front seat, when they both spun around with guns aimed after hearing gunshots.

Boom! Boom! Boom!

Gabe and Lorenzo saw Shantae standing a few feet away with her banger aimed. Then they noticed the body on the ground right behind the two of them. Gabe looked back at Shantae and met her eyes.

"That was the driver!" she told Gabe and Lorenzo. "Now hurry the fuck up!"

~ ~ ~

Brianna got the spot shut down once again for the second day and got away from the area and back to the penthouse. She stood out on the terrace and called Gabe's phone for the sixth time and still got no answer.

"Where the hell is he?" Brianna said aloud after hanging up on his voicemail. She tried calling

Lorenzo's phone and was surprised when he finally picked up.

"Yeah!"

"Lorenzo, where the hell is Gabe? Where the fuck did y'all go?"

"Relax, Brianna. We on our way to the apartment now!"

After hearing the line go dead in her ear, Brianna looked at the screen of her phone to see that Lorenzo had hung up the phone.

"That mutha!" Brianna started to say, but stopped after hearing the sliding glass door open behind her.

"Brianna!" Tamara called out to her as she walked out onto the terrace and handed her girl her cordless phone. "Erica's on the phone."

"What the hell does she want?" Brianna asked as she took the phone and placed it up to her ear.

"What?"

"Hello to you too, Brianna!" Erica said in the voice of someone smiling. "Listen! I want to meet tonight so we can discuss how things are going to be run!"

"Hell do you mean—?"

"Brianna, I'm not trying to argue with you!"

Erica spoke up, cutting her off. "Let's forget about our personal dislike and deal with business. I've spoken with my father, and he's agreed that as soon as I've learned how the business is run, I will be freed from dealing with you. So we can either make this a fast or slow process. Which do you prefer?"

Brianna sighed loudly into the phone. "Where the hell are we meeting, Erica?" she said after a brief moment.

~ ~ ~

Gabe used his keys and unlocked the front door to the penthouse and let himself inside. He was followed by Lorenzo, Shantae, Duke, and Boo Man. Gabe was barely inside when he heard Brianna's mouth.

"Gabe, where the hell have you and Lorenzo been? What in the fuck!" Brianna yelled as soon as her eyes landed on Gabe's ex-girlfriend. "Nigga, you must have really lost your damn mind! Why the fuck is that bitch in my house, Gabe?"

"Gabe, I'ma just wait—!"

Gabe held up his hand to stop Shantae from finishing what she was saying. He then held Brianna's eyes and saw her pissed-off expression. He told Lorenzo to take Shantae, Boo Man, and Duke into the den, and then he grabbed Brianna's arm and led her to the other side of the penthouse into their bedroom.

"Gabe, you need to start talking to me now!" Brianna demanded as she stood in the middle of the bedroom staring at Gabe as he began undressing.

"First, you need to learn how to talk to me, Brianna!" Gabe began as he walked into his closet and looked for something to change into.

"Excuse me?" Brianna yelled as she followed Gabe into his closet, where she stood beside him and faced him. "First of all, you need to remember who the hell your girlfriend is and learn some respect. How the hell you gonna bring that bitch into my fucking house?"

"First, her name is Shantae," Gabe got out before Brianna went off again.

He sighed as he gave up talking to her for the moment. He then grabbed a pair of blue metallic Polo jeans and a white-and-blue Polo pullover T-shirt and walked out of the walk-in closet with Brianna right behind him.

"Oh, so you gonna ignore me now, Gabe?"

Brianna asked as she stood behind him while he changed his clothes and still ignored her. "You know what! Fuck you, Gabe! I don't have time to deal with you and some young-ass bitch!"

Gabe shook his head as Brianna stormed out of the bedroom. He continued getting dressed to go out and see what Erica needed to talk to him about.

CHAPTER 6

G abe found Shantae, Boo Man, and Duke outside and standing in front of Duke's Range Rover. They were talking when Gabe stepped off the elevator into the parking garage. Gabe started walking toward his friends, when his cell phone began ringing. He dug out the phone and saw Brianna was on the line.

"Yeah, Brianna!"

"Baby, I'm sorry!" she said as soon as Gabe answered his phone. "Gabe, you're right! I shouldn't have been talking and treating you how I've been since you got back. It's just that since you left, I've been dealing with a lot by myself, and I've been under a lot of pressure. I love you, Gabe, and I'm sorry!"

Gabe sighed after listening to Brianna. He then looked up to meet Shantae's stare from a few feet away from her and the boys. He told Brianna he would be back up in a few minutes and then hung up the phone.

Gabe continued toward Shantae, Duke, and Boo Man. He barely stopped in front of the three of them when Shantae spoke up.

"We'll see you later, Gabe!" she told him, and then surprised both Duke and Boo Man when she kissed Gabe on his lips before turning to her brother and Boo Man and saying, "You two come on. We changing the plan until later!"

Gabe could see the questioning looks on the faces of Boo Man and Duke as to what Shantae had just told them.

"I gotta handle something, fam. We'll get up later!"

Gabe embraced Duke and Boo Man and then met Shantae's eyes as she stood beside her brother's Range Rover. He read her lips before she climbed into the SUV.

After Duke drove off, Gabe took the elevator back upstairs and got off on his floor. He used his keys and let himself into the front door and was closing it when Brianna rushed out of the den and straight over to him.

"I love you so much!" Brianna cried as she held onto Gabe tightly, hugging him around his neck as his arms went around her waist.

She then leaned back and passionately kissed him

on the lips.

~ ~ ~

"Shantae, you alright?" Duke asked his sister as he was pulling up in front of her condo a short while after leaving Gabe's place with his lady, Brianna.

"I'ma see you and Boo Man later!" Shantae told them as she was climbing from the back of the Range Rover.

She shut the back door to her brother's SUV and then walked up to the front door of her condo. She dug out her keys just as her cell phone began ringing again. She opened up her front door and then pulled her phone out.

"What the hell you want now, Tyree?"

"What the hell I want now?" Tyree repeated. "So that's how it's going to be between us now, huh?"

"Tyree, I already told you that it was over between us. So why are you still calling me then?"

"Shantae, it ain't going down like that, shorty!" he told her. "We been together too long to just up and end it for absolutely no fucking reason! I promise, if I find out you fucking with another—!"

"I am fucking with somebody else!" Shantae blurted out. "And believe me when I say that you best off just staying in your own lane. I'm going to say this one last time. Leave me the fuck alone!"

Shantae hung up the phone in her ex-boyfriend's face and then dropped onto the sofa in her den sighing deeply and loudly.

She picked up the phone again and called her best friend's number.

"Yeah!"

"Silk, where you at?"

"I'm at Rachell's house. What's up?"

"Never mind!"

"Where you at, Shantae?" he asked, cutting her off.

"Home!"

"I'm on my way over there now!"

"Bring something to smoke!" she told him before hanging up the phone.

~ ~ ~

Gabe was dressed and standing out on the terrace smoking a blunt that he had taken from Boo Man earlier. He was now talking to Nicole, who had called because she told him he was on her mind. Gabe was surprised when his step-mother suddenly asked him if he was in love with Brianna.

"Why'd you ask me that, Nicole?"

"Are you in love with Shantae, Gabriel, sweetheart?"

"Yeah, but we both know I'm with Brianna," Gabe explained. "What's up with all these questions though, Nicole?"

Nicole remained quiet for a few moments and sighed over the phone.

"Gabriel, sweetie, you need to make a decision before you hurt one of those women, or you end up being hurt yourself!"

"What are you talking about?"

"Gabriel, you may love Brianna and want to be with her, but you just admitted that you're in love with Shantae, and it's easy to see that you want to be with her. So why are you putting yourself through this growing problem?"

Gabe sighed as he leaned against the terrace's rail overlooking the ocean.

"Shantae messed up once before, Nicole!" he answered.

"But you told me yourself that you understood why she did what she did after you had some time to think about it; and to be truthful with you, sweetheart, I believe that girl really does love you!"

"So who would you want to see me with, Nicole?"

"I want to see you with who makes you happy, Gabriel."

"Baby, are you ready?" Brianna inquired as she pulled open the sliding glass door behind Gabe.

Gabe looked back at Brianna and stared at her for a moment. He then looked her over in her form-fitting skirt that reached mid-thigh level that perfectly hugged her curves. He told Nicole he would call her later.

"Okay, sweetheart. I love you, Gabriel!"

"Love you too, Nicole!" Gabe said before hanging up his phone.

"You ready to go, handsome?" Brianna asked as she ran her hand over the back of Gabe's wavy head.

After locking up the penthouse and leaving Duchess with Eddie, Gabe and Brianna took the elevator down to the garage and walked off toward Gabe's new Porsche.

"Baby, when did you buy this car?" Brianna asked Gabe after she got in and once Gabe got behind the wheel.

"I got it after I left this morning!" Gabe answered as he was backing out of his parking space.

"So what happened to the Buick and the Chevy Caprice?"

"I put 'em in storage!" he replied. "What's up with this visit out to Erica's spot?"

Brianna sucked her teeth and then said, "Erica's ass is talking about discussing how we're going to work things out. She's inviting us out to dinner with whatever new guy she's supposedly messing with now."

"Call her and let her know that we're on our way," Gabe told Brianna, even though he really wasn't trying to see or deal with Erica and her bullshit with Brianna tonight.

~ ~ ~

Erica smiled after hanging up the phone with Brianna. She stood at the mirror in front of her dresser inside her bedroom and was deep in thought when her phone began ringing again.

She looked down to see who was calling, and then picked up. "Where you at?"

"I'm just pulling into your building. Is everything ready?"

"Brianna just called, and she's just a few minutes away. Come on up through the front. The doorman knows you're coming."

After hanging up the phone and still smiling, Erica checked herself over once more in the mirror and then left her bedroom, ready for the night to begin.

~ ~ ~

Gabe and Brianna finally reached Erica's condo apartment and took the elevator up to her floor. Brianna led Gabe to her front door, only to hear what sounded like Trey Songz's "Dive In" playing inside.

Brianna knocked loudly to make sure it was heard over the music inside. She waited a few minutes and was just about to knock again when she heard the front door being unlocked.

"Brianna!" Anthony greeted, smiling after opening the door and seeing Brianna's shocked and surprised facial expression. "Erica's inside the kitchen. Come on in!"

Brianna was unable to believe what she was seeing. Brianna burst into the apartment, pushed past Anthony, and went to find Erica.

"Erica, what the hell is Anthony doing here?" she asked in a demanding voice, finding Erica seated at the breakfast bar drinking a glass of wine.

"Hello to you too!" Erica said to Brianna, smiling when Gabe and Anthony walked into the kitchen. "Gabe, you look good!"

"Baby, you ready?" Anthony asked, walking over and kissing Erica on her lips.

"I'm ready!" Erica replied as she stood up and picked up her Chanel bag, noticing the look on Brianna's face the whole time.

CHAPTER 7

After arriving at an Italian restaurant in Fort Lauderdale, Gabe parked the Porsche inside the very crowded, large parking lot. There was also a long line of people out front waiting to get inside. He and Brianna had been quiet since leaving Erica's apartment and were now walking to meet up with Erica and Anthony, who were standing waiting for them at the front of the restaurant.

"I hope you don't think we're about to wait out here in this long-ass line to get up into this shit, Erica!" Brianna said with much attitude as soon as she and Gabe walked up onto her and Anthony.

Erica smiled at Brianna but said nothing in response. She simply grabbed Anthony's hand and then led the group over to the front entrance to the restaurant.

Brianna was surprised when the men at the door spoke to Erica and knew her by name. They then opened the door and allowed Erica and her party to enter the restaurant. Brianna started to question Erica, only for the hostess to appear and address Erica by name, and then motion for their group to follow her.

"How the hell were you able to get us in here?" Brianna whispered to Erica as the four of them followed the hostess through the restaurant and past the live band up on stage in the corner.

"I know the owner!" was all Erica said, just as the hostess stopped at a U-shaped booth.

Once the four of them were seated and the menus were placed in front of them and the hostess walked off, Erica spoke up.

"So, what do you all think?"

"This is nice!" Anthony answered from Erica's right.

"How'd you get us in here, Erica?" Brianna asked her, all the while mean-mugging her step-sister.

"I told you, I know the owner!" Erica reminded Brianna. She then looked over at a quiet Gabe and asked, "What do you think, Gabe? Do you like it here?"

"It's nice, Erica," Gabe replied to her as he sat back looking around the place.

"Well, let's get this so-called meeting over with!" Brianna said, since she was already ready to leave and no longer wanted to be around Erica or Anthony's lying ass.

"Relax, Brianna!" Anthony told her, smiling over at her.

"Nigga, don't talk to me!" Brianna nastily shot back.

"So that's the way it is now, huh?" Anthony stated with a smile. "I figure we would have a better understanding after all we've shared together."

"Nigga, you better shut the fuck up now!" Brianna told him, raising her voice as her anger quickly raised.

"Miss Murphy!" a voice called.

Both Brianna and Erica turned as a medium-height Italian man walked up to their table escorted by two well-built men dressed in black suits.

"Mr. Galileo!" Erica said as she stood up from her seat, smiling as she embraced the middle-aged Italian man.

Erica then first introduced her Italian friend to Anthony, followed by Gabe and finally Brianna.

"I am not disappointed!" Mr. Galileo said, smiling flirtatiously at Brianna. "You're just as beautiful as your sister is, if not more. Please join me at my table."

"She's fine where she is!" Gabe spoke up in a tone that immediately drew everyone's attention to him.

Mr. Galileo smiled at the young man who was introduced as Gabriel Green. He then simply ignored Gabe and turned his attention back to Brianna.

"Miss Murphy, would you care to join me at my...?"

"What part of she's fine where she is don't you understand?" Gabe asked in a deadly-toned voice while sitting forward, which caused the two escorts to move forward. "You may want to continue speaking with Erica or head back to wherever you came from before things become bad real fast—really bad!"

Mr. Galileo chuckled at the threat that was made by the young man.

"I will excuse your small threat, young man!" he responded.

"It wasn't a threat!" Gabe stated, cutting off the Italian man. "I make promises that come true every time."

"Is that so, Mr. Green?" Mr. Galileo asked with

a smirk on his face.

Gabe ignored the man since he no longer had anything else to say and decided that it was time to leave. He took Brianna's hand.

"Bri, we're leaving!" Gabe said to her as he stood up, just as the one escort closest to him made the mistake of grabbing Gabe's arm.

Gabe moved before the escort or anyone else realized it. He broke the bodyguard's arm. Before the escort could yell out in pain, Gabe grabbed the back of his head, kicked in his right knee and broke it, and slammed the man's face down onto the table's edge so hard that part of it broke off.

"Pull it and I'll kill you where you stand, playboy!" Gabe told the other escort after peeping him reaching inside his suit coat.

He watched as the guy made a good decision to remove his hand from his coat pocket empty-handed.

"Bri, let's go!" Gabe reiterated while waiting until Brianna stood up from her seat.

The two of them then walked away from the table, ignoring the stares they were receiving as they left.

~ ~ ~

Smiling a bit and watching the young man as he walked away with Miss Murphy's step-sister, Mr. Galileo looked back at his escort who was laid out at his feet. He lay there unconscious with the front of his face busted open.

"Miss Murphy!" Mr. Galileo stated as he looked back at Erica, who stood smiling back at him.

"Was that not enough proof for you?" Erica asked the man. "I told you he was good!"

"He's better than good!" Galileo stated. "But it seems we have a problem considering how protective the young man is when it comes to your sister."

"Don't worry about that!" Erica told Mr. Galileo while still smiling. "I already have plans on how I will get Gabriel away from my step-sister once I tell him how unfaithful she was to him while he was away. Just be ready to deal with our agreement once I've held up my part of our deal."

~ ~ ~

After leaving the Italian restaurant, where Erica and Anthony remained, Gabe drove back to the penthouse. During the entire ride, Gabe and Brianna again remained silent.

Once they got home, Brianna headed to the

bedroom while Gabe went out onto the terrace to smoke a Newport.

"You okay?" Brianna asked some time later, sliding open the glass door and then walking outside to meet him.

She closed the glass behind her and then walked up behind Gabe, wrapping her arms around him from the back.

Gabe blew cigarette smoke up into the air as he felt Brianna kiss him on the neck.

"What's up with this clown-ass nigga, Anthony, Bri?"

"What do you mean?" she asked, releasing Gabe and stepping up beside him. She looked at him and asked, "What are you asking me, Gabe?"

After hearing how defensive Brianna got so quickly, Gabe looked over at her.

"What was all that stuff he was talking about you and him sharing so much shit together or something like that?"

"Gabe, what do you think he meant?" she asked with an attitude. "We used to date before you and me got together, remember?"

"Yeah, I remember!" Gabe answered, turning his

focus back out onto the water.

"Baby, you coming to bed with me?" she asked with a sigh after hearing how quiet Gabe got.

Gabe answered Brianna and told her that he wasn't ready to go to sleep yet, but that he'd be in a little bit later. He heard his cell phone ring and dug it out as Brianna walked back into the penthouse.

He saw that it was Erica on the line. He ignored the call only to hear the cell phone begin ringing again. It was Erica calling back.

"What, Erica?" he answered this time.

"I can't say that I was calling to see if you was okay after what you did to that guy at the restaurant. But I still want to make sure you're not upset with me."

"You good, Erica."

"You sure?"

"Yeah! You good!"

"How about you and Brianna? Are you two okay, Gabe?"

"Why wouldn't we be?"

"It just seems like you two seemed really upset with each other tonight. I was thinking I made a bad decision about bringing Anthony with us tonight considering what happened between them.

"Whoa!" Gabe said as he stood up straight after what he had just heard. "What the hell you mean something happened between Brianna and this nigga Anthony?"

"She didn't tell you, Gabe?"

"Erica, quit the bullshit, shorty! You and I both know you called me to tell me this shit. So get it the fuck off your chest and quit with the games!"

~ ~ ~

Shantae rolled over in her sleep and instantly fell out of the bed, waking up only to realize that she was not in her bed or bedroom at all, but on the sofa in the den. She had rolled off of it and onto the floor. She picked herself up and looked around, and then noticed that Silk was stretched out and asleep on the couch with his legs hanging off the end.

She remembered that the two of them had shared a good half a blunt, with the evidence in one of the ashtrays on top of her coffee table. She shut off the flat-screen television and then cleaned up her and Silk's mess. She walked into her bedroom and got an extra blanket and a pillow and tossed it onto the sofa in the den. She then went to work trying to wake up

Silk to move him from the smaller couch to the larger sofa.

"See you in the morning," she told Silk, who was already knocked back out as she was leaving the den.

After turning off the kitchen light, Shantae checked the locks on the front door, walked upstairs, and then started toward her bedroom. She was halfway there when her phone began to ring.

She looked at the phone while walking down the hallway toward her bedroom. Seeing who it was, she quickly answered the phone.

"Gabe!"

"Shantae, where you at?"

"Home. Why?"

"I'm down the street now! Come open the door!"

She heard the line end, which let her know that Gabe had hung up the phone. She turned around and headed back downstairs and out the front door. She stepped outside to wait for Gabe to show up.

Shantae instantly noticed the expression on Gabe's face as soon as he climbed out of the Porsche. She took his hand and then led him into her condo.

After locking the door behind them, Shantae led Gabe upstairs and down the hall to her bedroom. She closed the door behind them both.

"Let's lay down!" she told Gabe as she pulled off her T-shirt to show the white sports bra she had on.

She then pulled off her jeans but kept on the black and white tights she wore beneath them. She looked up to see that Gabe was still fully dressed and was sitting on the edge of her dresser with his head down deep in thought.

"Come on!" Shantae said as she helped Gabe out of his clothes down to his boxer briefs and wife beater he wore underneath.

She then led him over to her bed and got him into it and under the blanket.

Shantae set Gabe's Glock down on the dresser beside him and then walked around onto the far-right side, where she set her Glock atop the dresser beside her side of the bed. She climbed into bed beside Gabe afterward, only to have him roll over toward her, wrap his left arm across her middle, and lay his head on her breast.

After hearing his deep breathing and soft snoring after a few minutes, Shantae simply lay there holding him and rubbing the back of his head as he slept.

CHAPTER 8

S hantae was dreaming of making love with Gabe for the first time. She moaned in her sleep as Gabe first sucked on her right and then left nipple with a soft and gentle motion. He flicked his tongue across the tip, which caused her to arch her back and cry out his name.

She then felt him moving lower until he was positioned between her thighs and feeling his lips kiss her inner thighs. He then moved to the center. Just then, Shantae's eyes flew open when Gabe's lips made contact with her pussy.

"Gabe!" she cried out.

She then realized that she wasn't dreaming after looking down to see his head between her legs and his tongue working magic on her pussy.

"Baby!" Shantae cried, gripping his head as he slid his tongue deep inside her, playing with her clit.

"This belongs to me!" Gabe told her in between licks. "You belong to me, Shan!"

"Oh God!" Shantae could only cry out, pulling Gabe's head deeper into her as he attacked her clit, sucking just right. She heard herself screaming as she exploded into Gabe's mouth. "Gabe! Oh God! Yessss!"

Shantae was breathing so hard after cumming, but she still heard the tearing of something. She opened her eyes and looked up, only to find herself staring at Gabe rolling a condom over his dick, which was surprisingly much larger than she thought.

"Look at me!" Gabe told her as he positioned himself between her thighs. He lay down on top of her as they locked eyes with each other.

"You still love me, right?" Gabe asked after kissing Shantae's lips.

"I've always loved you, Gabe!" Shantae answered as she wrapped her arms up and around his neck.

Gabe reached down between the two of them and grabbed his manhood that was standing at its full nine and a half inches. He led just the head toward the opening of Shantae's womanhood.

Right before he was about to enter her, Gabe paused.

"If we do this, I need to know that I can trust you completely, Shan! If you with me, then that's how it's gonna be! I promise if I find any other nigga claiming you with him, I am going to really fuck somebody up. So be sure this is what you want!"

"After you're inside of me, you'll know for yourself that I'm all yours, Gabe! I've always been all yours!" Shantae told him, pulling him down to kiss his lips and feeling as he began pushing slowly inside of her.

~ ~ ~

Brianna woke up from the ringing of her cell phone and slowly opened her eyes. She first looked at the bedside clock and saw that it was almost noon. She then snatched up her still-ringing phone.

"Who the hell is this?"

"Brianna, what the hell is your problem? What the fuck have you done?"

Caught off guard, Brianna looked down at the phone screen and saw that it was Darrell on the line.

"Darrell, what are you talking about?" she asked as she sat up in bed.

"What the hell you mean 'what am I talking about?'" Darrell yelled. "Gabriel just called me a few moments ago and said he quits as your bodyguard and any other dealings with this family. What did you do?"

"I'll call you back!" Brianna said, hanging up the phone on Darrell while staring at the empty space in the bed where Gabe was supposed to be asleep.

Brianna climbed out of bed and quickly put on some shorts. She then walked out of the bedroom and rushed to the home gym where she expected to see Gabe, but only found an empty room.

Brianna left the gym and headed to the front of the penthouse still looking for Gabe. She relaxed a little after seeing Duchess with Eddie inside the kitchen. She asked her butler about Gabe, only to find out that he had not seen him that morning as well.

She grabbed her phone from the wall unit and walked from the kitchen into the den with Duchess trailing behind her. She dropped into the sofa as she listened to Gabe's cell phone go straight to voicemail.

~ ~ ~

"You a'ight?" Gabe asked Shantae for the fifth time since the two of them finished their love-making and were now inside the shower.

Shantae smiled as she leaned back from her position where she was laid up against Gabe's chest now to look into his eyes. She kissed him.

"Gabe, relax! I'm fine. And to be truthful, I feel better than I've ever felt!"

"So you're not in pain or anything?" he asked her.

"I'm a little sore, but I'm not gonna die, nigga!" Shantae told him, shaking her head and smiling. "You took my virginity. You didn't kill me, Gabe! Relax!"

"Why didn't you tell me that you was a virgin though?" he asked as she laid her head back onto his chest.

"Because, I wanted you to find out when you were ready!" Shantae told him. "Are you gonna tell me what happened last night and why you were so pissed off?"

Gabe remained quiet for a few minutes after hearing Shantae's story. He then sighed deeply and began explaining about him finding out about Brianna sleeping with her ex-dude while he was away training.

"Training for what?" Shantae asked him as they stood up together under the shower spray.

She kept quiet as Gabe broke down everything

about his agreement to work for Brianna's step-father as well as protect Brianna. He even got into the whole story of Brianna's father's killer being released from prison in a year or less.

"Gabe, wait!" Shantae told him once he paused in his story. "What you're telling me is the same story that was told to you by Brianna's step-sister and mother, right?"

"Yeah! Why?"

Shantae slowly shook her head while thinking over what Gabe had just told her.

"Gabe, something doesn't sound right about that whole story."

"What doesn't?"

"I'm not sure!" Shantae admitted, but then said, "Did you ask any questions about the guy who supposedly killed Brianna's father?"

"A few!" Gabe admitted. "Why? What you thinking, Shan?"

She remained quiet for a moment and then asked, "Gabe, what's this guy's name who killed Brianna's father?"

"I don't know!"

"Find out!" she asked him. "Something doesn't

sound or feel right about what you were just telling me with this whole thing."

"Shan, I'm just trying—!"

"Gabe, if this girl is really in danger, you just gonna let her get hurt or killed?" Shantae asked him, cutting him off. "Yeah, she may have cheated on you, but are you willing to let something happen to that girl after you promised to protect her?"

Gabe sighed out loud as Shantae stood staring at him and waiting for a reply.

"Alright! I'ma find out what this guy's name is, but how about telling me what you're up to?" he gave in.

"Find out the name first!" Shantae told him, kissing Gabe on the lips and then climbing out of the shower, leaving Gabe staring at her as she walked away. When she looked over her shoulder, she smiled catching him staring at her ass.

~ ~ ~

After they finished their shower together, Shantae put on a pair of dark blue Polo jeans, a white-and-blue fitted T-shirt, and a pair of brown Tims while Gabe put on his clothes that he had arrived in the night before: jeans, a wifebeater, and a pair of shoes.

They then decided to get something to eat before doing much of anything else. Shantae climbed into the passenger seat of Gabe's Porsche just as the ringing of his cell phone got her attention.

"You not going to answer that?" Shantae asked as Gabe was pulling off from in front of her condo.

He cut his eyes over to Shantae and shook his head as he dug out his cell phone to see that Brianna was calling.

"Yeah!" he answered.

"Gabe! Baby, where are you? I've been calling you all morning, and Darrell called and told me you said that you quit! What's going on?"

Gabe waited until Brianna was finished talking, and then asked, "Brianna, where you at now?"

"I'm home right now, but I'm about to go and handle something with Sherry and Tamara. Why you ask?"

"Go ahead and handle ya business, and let me know when you're heading home. I need to come by and pick up my stuff and grab Duchess."

"What? What are you talking about, Gabe?"

"We'll talk later, Brianna!"

Gabe hung up the phone even while Brianna was still talking. He tossed the phone onto the center console just as Shantae spoke up.

"So, you moving in with me, or are you getting your own place?"

"You offering?" Gabe asked, glancing over at Shantae.

"I don't need to!" Shantae told him with a smile. "You already know where I want you at. What are you gonna do though?"

"Let's talk about it while we eat!" he told her as he slowed the Porsche and turned into the parking lot at Denny's.

~ ~ ~

Brianna could not really focus on any business after her phone call with Gabe, hearing him tell her that he was packing his things and leaving. But she handled what she needed to and then met up with Erica and her new bodyguard at Olive Garden. Erica had called her earlier and wanted to talk business.

Brianna saw that Erica was already seated once she and Lorenzo arrived at the restaurant. Brianna stopped at the table and ignored the smile Erica had on her face.

"You're late, Brianna!" Erica said as her stepsister sat down across from her.

"And!" Brianna said with much attitude.

Erica was smiling and watching Brianna look through her menu that was in front of her, when she spoke up.

"I see Lorenzo is with you now. Where's Gabe at, Brianna?"

Brianna not only heard the question Erica had asked her, but she also noticed the way Erica asked it. She then lifted her eyes from the menu and looked over at a still-smiling Erica.

"Bitch, what did you do?" Brianna asked in her normal demanding voice.

Erica was lightly laughing after hearing Brianna's question. She picked up her own menu, only to have it snatched from her hands by Brianna.

"Bitch, do not play with me!" Brianna threatened, raising her voice.

Erica looked over to her right and saw Frank and Lorenzo on their feet. Both of them were staring at the other. Erica called to Frank and told him everything was okay. She then turned back to Brianna.

"You wanna know what I did? Just ask Gabe, and he'll tell you what we talked about last night."

"Bitch, do you really want me to fuck your stupid ass up?" Brianna yelled as she snatched up her Gucci bag and stood up from the table.

"By the way, Brianna!" Erica spoke up once more. "I decided Anthony wasn't really my type. But he asked me to tell you that since Gabe knows about you and him, for you to give him a call."

~ ~ ~

"Why didn't you tell me you knew that Silk was at the condo last night when you got here?" Shantae asked Gabe as the two of them were heading to meet up with Duke, Boo Man, Silk, and Silk's ladies, Rachell and Melody.

"I didn't know at first!" Gabe admitted, glancing from the road over to Shantae. "It wasn't until you fell asleep and I heard somebody use the bathroom that I walked up on Silk walking out."

"Gabe, please tell me you didn't go off and kick him out!" Shantae questioned, staring at Gabe with an expression of worry on her face.

"Naw! I ain't kick him out!" Gabe honestly told her before he told her how he and Silk actually chilled and did some talking and smoked a little.

"What y'all talk about?" Shantae asked.

"Mind ya business!"

"Boy, don't play with me!" Shantae told Gabe, punching him in the arm. "What did you two talk about?"

"Let's just say me and ya boy Silk got a better understanding of each other," Gabe explained, shooting a quick wink of the eye at Shantae, which caused her to smile and playfully roll her eyes at him.

~ ~ ~

After they made it out to Duke and Melody's condo apartment, Gabe and Shantae took the elevator up their floor and could hear DJ Khaled's "I Did It for My Dawgz" featuring Rick Ross, French Montana, and Jada coming from inside the condo. Shantae shook her head as she knocked on the door loud enough for them to hear.

"Hey, y'all!" Melody said with a smile after opening the front door.

She hugged Shantae first and then hugged her boo, wrapping her arms tightly around Gabe and holding him for a moment.

"What's good, Melody?" Gabe said once she

released him.

He smiled as she locked the door behind them, and then he laid his arm around her shoulders as they all headed to the den where everyone else was relaxing.

"Gabe!"

Gabe heard his name screamed out as soon as he and Melody got to the doorway of the den. He looked around just in time to see Gina leap up from the sofa beside a dark-skinned guy with braided hair. He released Melody just as Gina jumped up and wrapped her arms and legs around him.

"Bitch, I know you better get the fuck off of him!" Shantae spoke up before she realized it, and then stared hard at Gina.

Gina looked back at Shantae and saw that she was dead serious. Gina got down off of Gabe and then looked back and forth from Gabe to Shantae with a confused face.

"Umm, somebody wanna tell me what's going on?" Gina asked. "I thought you two were over!"

"Maybe you need to let the thinking be done by those who know how to!" Shantae told Gina as she walked over, sat down onto Gabe's lap, and lay back against his chest.

"Hold up!" Duke spoke up, shaking his head. "You two back together now?"

"Don't look surprised, nigga!" Shantae told her brother, showing a small smile as Gabe wrapped his right arm around her middle and then rested his hand on her thigh.

"It's about muthafucking time!" Boo Man spoke up, drawing all the others' attention over to him.

"Tamara!" Gabe called out when he noticed her sitting next to Boo Man.

"Hey, Gabe!" she said with a smile and a little wave to him.

"Wait!" Gabe said, looking from Tamara to Boo Man and back to Tamara. "You and Boo Man are kicking it, T?"

Tamara nodded her head in response and then said, "I've been seeing Boo Man since you left for your training in Tokyo."

"Damn!" Gabe said with surprise at what he was just now finding out. "I ain't even know about this!"

"None of us did, fam!" Duke added. "They kept it on the low until now!"

"Well, I guess this is a welcome to the family

then!" Gabe told Tamara, getting a bigger smile from her.

"Well, now that we are all here," Silk started, getting everyone's attention. "We heading out tonight or what?"

"That's the plan!" Duke said. "What's up, Gabe? You and Shantae going to roll with us tonight or what?"

"What time y'all trying to leave?" Shantae asked. "Gabe has something to handle in a little while. So we need to know what time, so we'll be ready."

"How about 11:00 or 11:30 p.m.?" Duke asked, looking around at the others and seeing the nods of agreement.

He then looked back at Gabe and Shantae.

"What's up, babe?" Shantae asked, looking back at Gabe.

"Hold up!" he replied, patting Shantae on the butt for her to get up. He stood up and then pulled out his cell phone as he walked out of the den.

As soon as Gabe walked out of the room, Melody and all the other girls rushed Shantae. They all wanted to know what was really up with her and Gabe.

~ ~ ~

Gabe was standing outside on the terrace at Duke and Melody's condo. He then got on the phone with Brianna.

"Baby, where are you?" Brianna asked as soon as she answered the phone. "Gabe, we really need to talk. I don't know what the hell Erica told you, but I can explain!"

"Where you at, Brianna?"

"I just got home."

"A'ight! I'ma be there in a few minutes."

"Gabe, I love you!"

"I'll see you in a few minutes, Brianna."

After hanging up on Brianna after she was still talking, Gabe stood up for a few moments, when he became aware that he was being watched.

He looked back over his shoulder to see Tamara standing on the other side of the sliding glass door. He motioned her outside with him.

"Hey, Gabe!" Tamara said after sliding open the door and stepping out onto the terrace with him.

"What up, T?" Gabe replied as Tamara walked up beside him. "I guess you wanna know what's up, huh?"

"Actually, I already know," Tamara admitted as she turned to face Gabe. "I figured when you found out about Anthony that you would leave her, Gabe."

"So, you knew about those two then?"

Tamara nodded her head.

"I've known Brianna and Anthony for a long time, and those two been off and on for years. The problem between those two is that Anthony's too weak. That's why she was so attracted to you. But being truthful with you, Gabe, I'm happy you found out. I really fell in love with you as someone would a real close friend; and after getting to know you, I hated that you were messing with Brianna. Don't get me wrong: Brianna's my girl, and I love her, but I don't like how she was treating you, and I've heard about you and Shantae. You two actually make a sexy couple anyway."

"So we cool, right?" Gabe asked her.

Tamara hugged Gabe after answering his question. She then kissed his cheek just as the sliding glass door was pulled open.

"Am I interrupting?" Shantae asked, looking from Gabe to Tamara and then back to Gabe with a questioning look on her face.

"You know, Gabe!" Tamara started, looking back at him and smiling. "Now that I think about it, she actually reminds me a lot of you with her attitude and quick temper."

"Yeah!" Gabe said with a grin. He then looked back at Shantae and winked at her. "I'm noticing that too!"

CHAPTER 9

Gabe finally made it out to the penthouse using Duke's Range Rover with Boo Man and Duke rolling with him while Silk drove. Gabe led his boys up the elevator and to Brianna's place. He stepped off the elevator once the doors opened. He used the keys that Brianna had given him, and he let himself and the boys inside, only to hear Duchess barking. He saw her running toward him from the other side of the apart-ment.

"Hey, baby girl!" he said as he squatted down to accept an excited Duchess as she leapt into his arms.

"I hope you're just as happy to see me too!" Brianna said to Gabe as she walked into the front room.

Gabe lifted his eyes to meet Brianna's gaze. He then shook his head sadly as he stood back up.

"Boo! Duke!" Gabe called as he was looking back at his boys. "Y'all leave the den how it is, but I'm taking the stereo. Then start working on the weight room. Get all you can get, and I'll come back for the rest later."

"So, you're really leaving?" Brianna asked as she

followed behind Gabe as he headed to the other side of the apartment.

Gabe didn't have anything to say, so Brianna followed him into the bedroom.

"So that's it, huh? You're just gonna leave without talking to me about what's wrong, Gabe?" she asked.

"What's the use of talking?" Gabe told her as he began packing up his things that he was taking. "You know just as I do that there's really nothing left to talk about when you had all the time you needed to tell me about the bullshit that you and that clown Anthony had or have going on."

"Gabe, it's not what you—!"

"Let your step-father know I'm still finishing with our business dealings; and until things are figured out with your father's killer, I'll be there if you need me. I won't go back on my promise to protect you!"

"So that's it?" Brianna asked as she stood staring angrily at him. "You just gonna turn your back on us, Gabe? I thought you loved me?"

Gabe paused in his packing and turned his full attention to Brianna.

"Did yo' ass think about that shit when you had that punk-ass nigga between ya legs licking and eating ya pussy, or all the other times you had that nigga getting the pussy you kept claiming was for me, huh?"

"Gabe, that was—!"

"I'm done with that shit!" Gabe told her, raising his voice and shocking Brianna for a few moments before she started going off.

Gabe ignored Brianna by this point and continued packing his bags. He was packing up his bangers when she made the promise to fuck up the first bitch that she saw him with. Gabe opened his mouth to respond to her threat, but he decided against it and just continued what he was doing.

~ ~ ~

Shantae tried not to watch the clock, but she was unable to help it. She was supposed to be kicking it with Melody and the other girls. She shifted her eyes and looked at the wall clock, and saw that it was almost two hours since Gabe, Duke, Boo Man, and Silk left to go and pick up Gabe's things from Brianna's place.

"Fuck this!" Shantae announced as she began

pulling out her cell phone at the same time the front door opened and a laughing Gabe, Duke, Boo Man, and Silk walked into the condo apartment.

"Happy now?" Melody asked as she walked past Shantae, smiling and shaking her head at the girl.

"What up, ma?" Gabe said as he walked into the den and over to Shantae. He bent down and kissed her on the lips. "You ready to head home and get ready?"

Shantae nodded her head yes and stood up from the sofa as Gabe dropped his arm around her shoulders.

"Yo, is we meeting up back here or at this club you all was talking about?" Gabe asked before he and Shantae left.

"Shantae knows where Club Static is at," Duke replied. "We'll meet at the front door at 11:30."

"We'll see y'all at 11:30 p.m. then," Gabe repeated as he escorted Shantae out of the apartment.

Duke locked the door after Gabe and his sister walked out, and he then looked back at Melody.

"That girl is crazy about that boy, Duke!" she said.

"Oh, I've noticed!" Duke replied to her, smiling

at the thought of his boy and his sister together.

After leaving Duke and Melody's building, Gabe drove away, and within minutes, Shantae began questioning him.

"So, what happened?" Shantae asked. "Did she act up when you was leaving?"

Gabe shook his head and answered, "Just a lot of shit talking, but I want you to stay away from her!"

"Why you say it like that?" Shantae asked while staring at Gabe.

He explained to her about Brianna's threat and how he felt about it, considering who she really was and who her family was. Gabe then saw that Shantae understood what he was telling her. After glancing over at her, he noticed something else that didn't surprise him at all, which was her anger.

Once at Shantae's condo, Gabe parked beside her Audi RS7. He shut off the engine and the two of them got out and headed up to the front door.

"What the fuck?" Shantae said, leaping back after opening the front door and seeing the muscular dog that stood on the other side.

"Duchess, sit!" Gabe told his girl. He then looked at Shantae with a smirk and said, "Relax, ma! This is my baby girl, Duchess."

"What the fuck, Gabe!" Shantae said as she kept a close eye on the dog. "Why the fuck didn't you tell me that thing was inside my shit?"

"Come here, ma!" Gabe told Shantae, reaching for her hand only to have her snatch it away.

"Nigga, don't touch me!" Shantae told Gabe, only to have him ignore her and pull her up against him.

"Just relax, Shantae!"

"Gabe, I'm telling you now, nigga. If that dog bites me, I'ma shoot it and then I'ma shoot your ass too!"

Gabe laughed at her threat and called Duchess. She walked from out of the condo and over to where he and Shantae stood.

"Hold ya hand out with your palm up, Shantae!" he told her.

"Hell no, nigga!" Shantae told Gabe in fear, only to have him pull her down into a squat position with him. He held her tight as he called the dog over to them. "Gabe, I'm telling yo' ass—!"

"Relax!" Gabe told her as Duchess began sniffing Shantae's hand before she got closer and began licking it. "See what I told your sorry ass!"

"Shut up, punk!" Shantae told him, punching Gabe in his chest.

~ ~ ~

They showered together thinking they would save time; however, they ended up spending longer than planned inside making love. Gabe and Shantae finally made it out of the shower and had to rush getting dressed to be out of the house before 11:00 p.m.

Gabe dressed in black metallic Gucci jeans, a cream and tan Gucci shirt, a tan jacket, and all-white Air Force One low-tops. Gabe then stood outside on the front porch smoking a Newport and waiting for Shantae to finish getting ready, when his cell phone began ringing.

"What up, Erica?" Gabe answered after seeing her name appear across the screen of his phone.

"Are you busy?"

"At the moment, no! What's up?"

"I need to talk with you."

"I'm listening."

"Not over the phone, Gabe. Can you come to my place so we can talk?"

"How about we meet some place like a restaurant or a park?"

"Are you afraid to be alone with me, Gabe?"

"I'm afraid what may happen to you if my girl finds out about you trying to be alone with me!" Gabe told Erica truthfully. "Call me tomorrow, Erica. We can meet at Scott Park at twelve noon."

"I'll see you then, Gabe!"

After hanging up with Erica, Gabe barely lowered the phone from his ear, when he heard a throat being cleared loudly.

"I'm not even gonna ask who that was you're planning to meet tomorrow," Shantae told him, walking behind Gabe and over to the Porsche.

Gabe had a smirk on his face as he stood watching Shantae as she walked off. He then shifted his eyes lower and past her small waist to her swaying hips and ass that sat up inside the jeans she was wearing. He couldn't help but notice the change in her that seemed even more sexy to him.

"You plan on standing there staring, or are we leaving?" Shantae asked, smiling after looking back and catching Gabe staring at her ass.

CHAPTER 10

G abe was not at all surprised to see how crowded Club Static was after hearing how well known it was. He found an open space to park, and then he and Shantae walked back up the street and headed for the front entrance to the crowded club.

"Ain't that Duke and them right there?" Shantae asked, pointing in the direction she saw her brother and what looked like the others.

Gabe saw where Shantae was pointing, so he followed alongside her as she basically led the way through the crowded parking lot, until his hand was grabbed.

"Damn, sexy! Where you going?" a cute brown-skinned female asked after stopping Gabe. "What's your name, boy?"

"Serious problems!" Shantae spoke up as she stepped in between Gabe and the female, facing the girl. "You may wanna keep ya hands to yourself before it earns you a free trip to the emergency room!"

"What!" the female said, looking Shantae over

like she was stupid. She then turned back to her girls and said, "Y'all hear this bitch?"

"I know I heard her!" Tamara said as she walked up to stand beside Shantae. "And I'm pretty sure she gave you the only warning you're going to get before you find out how long that trip gonna be before you get to the emergency room."

"Bitch, who the—!"

"A'ight, enough!" Gabe finally spoke up, grabbing Shantae and Tamara. "It's time to go, you two!"

Gabe led both loose cannons away before either Shantae or Tamara turned shit up before the night even really started.

"Where the hell you come from?" Gabe asked Tamara.

"Boo left something inside the truck!" Tamara informed Gabe before she turned back to Shantae asking about what had just happened.

They hooked up with Duke, Melody, and all the others, only for Tamara and Shantae to instantly get straight into the bullshit that almost just popped off a few minutes earlier. Gabe and Duke then got the group moving while Boo Man and Silk were the ones that got everyone past security at the door.

Once they stepped inside the club, Shantae found her way beside Gabe as the group then headed through the crowded elbow-to-elbow-packed club and made their way over to one of the bars.

"Shantae, come on, girl!" Tamara said, grabbing her hand. "Let's walk around and see who's here!"

"Hold on, girl!" Shantae told Tamara and the other girls, turning back to face Gabe. She walked up to her man and kissed him directly on his lips and said, "I hope you don't have me up in here tonight acting a damn fool!"

"Remember them same words!" Gabe told her, slapping her on the ass as she turned to walk away, earning him a smile that she gave back over her shoulder as she, Melody, Tamara, Rachell, and Gina disappeared into the crowd.

~ ~ ~

Tyree saw Shantae as soon as she entered the club with the group. He instantly felt a certain way after seeing his bitch kissing up on some pretty boy punk muthafucker. Tyree gripped the rail as he stood in the VIP area and watched Shantae and the four other females that were with her now walking through the club.

"Ty, what's up?" Rambo asked as he and Worm walked up onto his left and right side. "Why you over here with your face all balled up, my nigga!"

"I see this bitch Shantae up in his shit!" Tyree told his boys, pointing her out down below. "She up in this shit with some soft-ass pretty muthafucker!"

"So what's up?" Worm asked. "You getting at the bitch or what?"

Tyree looked over at Worm but ignored his comment. In fact, he took the fat muthafucker's advice and pushed away from the rail.

"You niggas coming?" Tyree asked as he started toward the steps to leave the VIP section.

~ ~ ~

Shantae and the girls kicked it with some other girls they knew. She then stood talking with one guy that she and Silk used to chill with until he got locked up and ended up heading to prison.

"When you get out, Stick?" Shantae asked him, taking the blunt that Stick had passed over to her.

"I got out two days ago!" he replied. "What's good with you and my nigga Silk? Y'all still doing ya thing?"

"Not like we used to, but Silk's up in here now too!" Shantae told her friend. "He's with Boo Man and my boyfriend."

"Whoa!" Stick said with a smile. "You say what? You got a dude now, Shantae?"

"Nigga, don't sound so surprised!" she said, just as she was snatched around suddenly to find herself face-to-face with her ex-boyfriend.

"Bitch, what the fuck you doing up in here?" Tyree questioned, getting all up into Shantae's face. "And who the fuck is that punk-ass nigga I saw you kissing all up on?"

"Nigga, get the fuck off of me!" Shantae yelled, snatching away from Tyree after the shock faded. "I already told your begging ass to leave me!"

Shantae was unable to finish what she was saying when Tyree slapped the shit out of her. She reacted by throwing a quick three-piece that caught Tyree by surprise and staggered his ass backward, only to have him gain his control and rush back at her.

She snatched up the Corona bottle that she saw on the bar, and swung and smashed it across the side of Tyree's head, dropping him to his knees. She was grabbed, just when Tamara and her girls ran over to help her.

~ ~ ~

Gabe laughed at Boo Man's crazy ass when the commotion broke out. He and the rest of his boys all looked in the direction of the gathering crowd and saw some type of fight that was going on.

"Yo, ain't that Shan—?"

Gabe peeped Shantae just as Gina's dude was talking. He took off from the guys at the bar and was pushing through the crowd. He even elbowed a guy who decided to grab him. He actually broke homeboy's nose and was already moving again before the guy could begin screaming.

He pushed straight through the crowd and into the center of the club where the fight was going on. Gabe's eyes locked in on the dark-brown-skinned dude fighting with Shantae and bleeding from the side of his head.

Gabe moved just as Duke and the others appeared at his side. Gabe ran up onto homeboy, just as he was swinging at Shantae. Gabe caught Tyree's arm in mid-air, and within seconds he had his arm folded backward and broken.

Moving again, Gabe landed a well-placed side

kick that shot between Tamara and Melody to connect with the face of the fat dark-skinned guy with whom the two of them were fighting. He then swung his attention to the third guy, who pushed Rachell down and threw Gina down off his back.

Gabe hooked his foot under a stool at the bar and sent it flying at homeboy just as the guy turned around, only to see the stool smash the guy directly in the face and knock his ass into the crowd behind him.

Gabe turned his attention back to Shantae and saw the blood on her lip. He walked over to her, with his anger building the closer he got. There was also blood running down from under her left eye.

Shantae saw the look on Gabe's face just as he looked down at Tyree, who was crawling toward a table. She saw what was about to happen, just as Gabe started walking in Tyree's direction.

"Gabe!" she yelled, rushing toward him and grabbing him. "Babe, that's enough! Let's just get out of here before the police show up!"

"Fam, Shantae's right!" Duke told Gabe. "Bruh, you really fucked these guys up! We need to get the hell out of here! Now!"

Gabe looked back at the homeboy with whom Shantae had been fighting. He then allowed her to lead him away from the scene.

~ ~ ~

Once they were outside the club, the group headed toward where they were parked. Gabe gave Shantae the keys.

"Go to the car, Shantae!" he told her.

He started to turn away, but she grabbed his arm.

"Gabe, what are you gonna do?" she asked, seeing the silent anger on his face.

"Go to the car, Shan!" he repeated before turning and walking away.

Gabe saw Boo Man's Escalade pull around to the exit first. Gabe stopped his boy and walked around to the passenger side.

"What's wrong, Gabe?" Tamara asked after letting down the window.

"Tamara, I need you to go with Shantae right now!" Gabe ordered her. "I need to use ya man's help!"

Tamara asked no questions. She kissed Boo Man before getting out of the SUV and rushing off to catch up with Shantae. Tamara could only imagine what was about to happen.

~ ~ ~

Gabe waited and watched until both the paramedics and Miami PD finally arrived to pick up homeboy and his boys who got into it with Shantae and the other girls. Gabe kept his eyes locked on the stretcher that had the guy who was fighting with Shantae on it.

"Follow that first truck!" Gabe told Boo Man once the paramedic truck pulled out of the club's parking lot.

"You got ya banger in here with you?" Gabe asked Boo Man.

"There's one in there, fam!" Boo Man informed Gabe, nodding toward the glove compartment.

Gabe checked inside and found a chrome .40 caliber. He checked the magazine and saw that the piece was fully loaded. He slid the clip back into the gun and then sent a round into the chamber.

"Bruh, just what are you about to do?" Boo Man asked Gabe, seeing the look on his man's face.

"Speed up, fam!" Gabe told Boo Man while letting back down the passenger window while also ignoring his boy's questions.

Gabe swung his right arm out the window while holding the .40 caliber in his hand. He then aimed the gun.

Boom! Boom!

Gabe blew out the back tires of the paramedic truck, which caused the speeding truck to lose control and slam into a light pole. The truck then spun off about two feet into the middle of the street.

"What the fuck!" Boo Man called out in disbelief.

"Stop the truck!" Gabe told Boo Man as the Escalade was flying past the paramedics' truck.

"What?" Boo Man asked, shooting Gabe a look.

"Boo, stop the fucking truck!" Gabe demanded again in a tone that Boo Man understood this time.

"I'll be right back!" Gabe told his boy once the big man stopped the Escalade.

Gabe climbed out of the truck and then started to walk in the direction of the paramedic truck.

~ ~ ~

"You a'ight, Shantae?"

She looked back at Tamara as she stood inside the doorway back at the condo. Shantae shook her head as she looked back out at the streets in front of her condo.

"I wanna know where the hell Gabe is!"

"If that's what's worrying you, then don't!" Tamara told her. "Gabe is fully capable of handling situations like these. Trust me! I've seen the reports on his training that he spent a year and some months going through in order to protect Brianna and handle issues for Darrell, Brianna's father."

"I keep hearing about this training!" Shantae stated as she turned to face Tamara. "What type of training did Gabe go through?"

"Let's just say that if Gabe was ever labeled, he would be called an assassin because of all the stuff he now knows how to do."

Shantae stared at Tamara in disbelief after what she had just learned. Shantae started to ask a question, when her cell phone began ringing from inside her pocket.

She saw that Melody was on the line, so she answered the call, albeit a bit disappointed that it was not Gabe.

"Yeah, Melody?"

"Shantae, is Gabe there with you?"

"No, girl, why?" she asked when she heard the

tone in Melody's voice. "What happened, Melody?"

"Shantae, turn on the news, girl!"

"What the fuck's going on, Melody?" Shantae asked again as she rushed into the condo with Tamara right behind her.

"Just turn to channel 7, Shantae!"

Shantae did as Melody asked, and stared at the live news report concerning a paramedic truck being attacked and leaving three paramedics seriously injured and unconscious. The reporter went on to explain that paramedics and police were on the scene assisting the injured. However, the initial injured person being taken to the hospital was found shot once in the head execution style.

Shantae dropped the remote and almost fell to the floor once the name of the murdered passenger was announced, had Tamara not caught her. She then allowed Tamara to help her to a seat on the sofa while still listening to the news report.

"I can't believe this!" Shantae exclaimed after the news report finished. She looked over at Tamara sitting across from her. "That was—!"

"I know!" Tamara said, cutting her off. "Melody just told me who the guy was. I know, Shantae!"

~ ~ ~

Shantae was unsure when she fell asleep, but she slowly awoke as she was being laid down in her bed. In the dark, she made out Gabe, who was pulling off his shirt.

"Gabe!" Shantae said, calling to him in a lowered tone.

"Yeah, Shan!" he answered, glancing back at her as he was looking for a new pair of boxer briefs and a wifebeater.

"I saw the news!" Shantae told him, meeting Gabe's eyes once he looked back at her. "I know why you did it. Tamara explained it to me. Thank you, Gabe."

Gabe said nothing at first. He simply turned back toward the bed, walked over, and bent down and kissed Shantae on the lips.

"I know who he was to you, Shantae. I also know you ended things with him and what was happening with him, but it doesn't matter now!" he whispered to her.

Shantae watched Gabe as he walked off and headed to the bathroom. She called out to him to get his attention.

"I love you, Gabe!"

"You promise?"

"Do I need to prove it?"

Gabe gave her a small smile when he looked over his shoulder and replied, "Prove it to me tomorrow."

Shantae smiled after Gabe winked at her before he walked into the bathroom. She then closed her eyes and sighed as she wondered what exactly Gabe was planning for tomorrow.

CHAPTER 11

Gabe and Duke ignored all the stares they were receiving due to Shantae and Melody running through the lobby of the downtown courthouse. Both men followed behind their women, only to burst out laughing when the saw the two of them already in the parking lot on their phones, most likely telling everyone they knew that they were just married.

"Fam, everything set up at the dealership?" Duke asked as he and Gabe followed Shantae and Melody out into the parking lot, with both girls on their phones.

"Yeah!" Gabe replied, smiling and watching his new wife. He then looked over at Duke and said, "The homeboy at the dealership sent me a text a little earlier. He said everything's all set to go."

Gabe reached Duke's Range Rover where Melody and Shantae stood together talking on their phones. Gabe met his wife's eyes and received a smile and then a kiss.

"I love you!" Shantae told Gabe, holding the phone away from her lips to tell him. "You do know my mom wants us to come over, right?"

"I figured that!" Gabe stated as he climbed into the back of the Range Rover right behind Shantae.

"Duke, Momma wants us to come by the house," she informed her brother while texting Tamara.

"Yeah, alright!" Duke answered as he was backing out of his parking spot. "We gotta handle something first!"

"Handle what?" both Shantae and Melody said together as they both looked up from their phones.

"Y'all just relax!" Gabe spoke up. "Y'all will find out in a little while."

~ ~ ~

"Duke, what the hell are we doing at the Bentley dealership?" Melody asked her husband after realizing where they were turning. However, Duke simply ignored his wife and parked the Range Rover in the parking lot.

"Gabe!" Melody said as the four of them all got out of the SUV. She grabbed his arm to get his attention. "What's going on? What are you and Duke up to?"

"You'll see!" was all Gabe told her as he dropped his right arm across her shoulders before he began leading his wife from the parking lot into the dealership.

Once the four of them were inside, Gabe walked off after telling them that he would be right back. He left Duke to deal with the women.

"Duke, what's going on?" Melody asked him again. "Why are we here?"

"You'll see!" Duke told her as he continued looking around, ignoring the way she was staring at him but noticing Shantae had nothing to say.

"Duke!"

After hearing his name a few moments later, Duke turned around to see Gabe and a dark-haired white guy with square-frame glasses dressed in a navy-blue suit. He knew instantly that the white man had to be the guy who Gabe had told him about.

Gabe introduced Greg Curry to everyone and then explained to the girls and Duke that the salesman was responsible for making sure everything was set up for the four of them. Gabe never got the chance to finish what he was saying when Melody interrupted.

"Ummm, excuse me. Mr. Curry, right?" Melody called out. "Can you explain to me exactly what's going on here, please?"

Greg had a big smile on his face and said, "Mrs. Mitchell, how about I show you and Mrs. Green what is it that Mr. Mitchell and Mr. Green have for the two of you. Follow me, if you would, please."

Melody shot Duke and then Gabe a look, and then grabbed Melody's hand. She then followed the salesman and ended up outside walking around to the back side of the dealership until all five of them were together.

"Tell me what you think, ma?" Gabe said, whispering into Shantae's ear.

"Here we go!" Greg stated, waving his hand as the he-and-she 2018-model Bentley GT Speeds were pulled around in front of the group. The salesman looked back at Gabe and said, "Mr. Green, here are your and Mrs. Green's cars, sir."

"Oh my God!" Melody cried in disbelief as she stood staring at the glacier-white Bentley and the blue-crystal Bentley that were the exact same models.

"Which one, ma?" Gabe asked, smiling as he looked at Shantae.

"I like the blue one!" she replied as she walked over to the salesman standing in front of the blue-crystal Bentley and took the keys that he was holding out for her.

She opened the driver's door and climbed inside onto the dark bourbon leather seats. While Shantae sat down and began looking around at the interior, she suddenly heard someone begin to scream.

She hopped out of the car and reached for her Glock, only to instantly notice the twin-model Bentley Bentaygas that were pulling up. Shantae smiled as she stood watching Melody take off running toward one of the SUVs.

"Would you rather have the truck over the car?" Gabe asked from behind Shantae at the end of the Bentley GT Speed.

Shantae shook her head.

"Hell no! I'm in love with my new car!"

"Good!" Gabe replied, winking at her.

~ ~ ~

After leaving the Bentley dealership and heading across town to their mother's house, Gabe explained that he had a meeting that he needed to attend, but he promised to tell her about it once he returned. Shantae slowed the Bentley GT Speed in front of her mother and step-father's house and wasn't surprised to see the crowd that was standing in their front yard. Shantae parked the car and opened the door, just as Michelle, Gina, and a few of her other friends ran up to the car.

"Bitch, whose car is this?" Michelle asked, pushing Shantae out of the way and looking into the Bentley. "Girl, this is bad, Shantae!"

"Shantae, where's my boo at?" Gina asked, to which she received a look and dismissive wave from Shantae. "Girl, OMG! That's your man, but I still love me some fine-ass Gabriel Green!"

"I wanna see the ring, girl!" another friend yelled out, grabbing Shantae's hand to examine the matching rose-gold engagement ring and wedding ring that had a square-cut chocolate diamond that was as big as Shantae's thumb. "Damn! I ain't know Gabe was paid like this, Shantae!"

"Shantae Mitchell!"

Shantae immediately recognized her mother's voice. She looked up at the front porch and saw her mother with Duke and Melody. She walked away from her friends and up onto the porch to greet her mother.

"Hi, Momma!

"Hi, baby!" Ms. Mitchell cried out happily, throwing her arms around her only daughter. "Shantae, I'm so happy for you, baby!"

Shantae returned her mother's hug and then locked eyes with her best friend, Silk, standing to the left of her mother. She returned the smile that he was giving her.

"Shantae, where's my son-in-law at now?" Ms. Mitchell asked while looking at the big diamond ring her daughter had on her ring finger.

"You already know how Gabe is, Momma! His butt is in the middle of something right now!" she told her as she was getting ready to hug Silk.

~ ~ ~

Gabe was sitting on a park bench for about ten minutes. He then looked up and watched as the S550 Mercedes-Benz Executive pulled up in front of the parking lot at the entrance to Scott Park. He continued to watch the Benz as Frank climbed from behind the wheel and opened the back door for Erica to step out.

Gabe tossed his cigarette butt to the ground as he watched Erica and Frank head in his direction. He sat back against the bench as Frank stopped in front of him and Erica made herself comfortable beside Gabe.

"Don't let what's on ya mind get you fucked up real bad, big homie!" Gabe told Frank, staring up at the big guy.

"Frank!" Erica spoke up, seeing the look on her bodyguard's face. "Wait for me at the car until I'm finished with Gabe."

Gabe smirked watching an obviously upset Frank walk off as he was told, and then he turned back to Erica.

"Erica, you better talk with ya bodyguard before you end up running an ad in the newspaper for a new one!"

"Frank doesn't bother you, does he, Gabe?" Erica asked as she laid her hand onto his left thigh and rubbed it up and down.

"What do you wanna talk to me about, Erica?" he asked as he removed her hand from his leg.

"I want to talk to you about a business deal I've had in mind for us!" Erica said with a big smile.

"Us?"

"Yes!"

"What are you getting at, Erica?" Gabe

questioned as he dug out his vibrating cell phone to see that he had a text message.

"Are you in a hurry, Gabe?" Erica asked him, seeing him look down at his stylish watch, of which she was unsure of the high-end brand.

"You've got fifteen minutes, and then I gotta go!" he explained to her. "So talk!"

She nodded her head after noticing the sudden change in Gabe, so she got straight to the point.

"I'm sure you remember Mr. Galileo from the other night. But what you didn't get the chance to find out before you left was that he wanted to offer you a position."

"Position on what?" Gabe asked her.

"Well, Mr. Galileo is planning to go into business with my father, and he wants to hire you as his—!"

"Not interested!" Gabe stated, cutting off Erica as she was in the middle of explaining. "Is there something else you wanna talk to me about?"

"Gabe, will you just hear me out?" Erica asked as he stood up from the bench.

"I'm not interested in anything dealing with your father or your Italian friend, who I really didn't like the last time me and homeboy met. But I gotta go!"

Erica remained sitting where she was as Gabe walked away and over to his gorgeous new Bentley. She noticed the way Frank stared at Gabe, and she couldn't help but smile.

"You ready to go, Miss Murphy?" Frank asked as he walked over to her.

Erica held up her hand for a moment for Frank to hold on as she made a quick phone call. She listened as her phone began to ring.

"Hello!"

"Mr. Galileo. This is Erica."

"Hello, Miss Murphy. How did the meeting go with our friend?"

"We have a problem again."

~ ~ ~

Shantae hung out on the front porch with Silk, Duke, and the others while her mother and Melody's mother were inside the kitchen planning a dinner. Shantae looked over at Boo Man, who had arrived a little while ago with Tamara. She took the blunt that he held out for her, just as her cell phone woke up, ringing from inside her back pocket.

"That's gotta be Gabe!" Melody said, seeing the smile that suddenly appeared on Shantae's face.

"Hey, babe!" Shantae said into the phone, still smiling as she rolled her eyes at Melody. "Where you at?"

"I just picked up Nicole! You still at your mom's house?"

"Everybody's over here! My mom's been asking about you, and both my mom and Melody's mom are planning on cooking dinner for us."

"Hold up!"

Shantae stood up and could hear Gabe's voice lightly on the other end of the line talking with his step-mother. Shantae then passed the blunt to her right to Silk, just as Gabe came back on the line.

"Shan!"

"Yeah, babe!"

"Find out what Ms. Mitchell and Ms. Jackson need. I'ma stop at Walmart or someplace for the food!"

"You talk to her!" Shantae told her husband as she went into the house to give the phone to her mother.

CHAPTER 12

G abe looked at Shantae as she lay against him fast asleep as they all sat in the front room of her and Duke's mother's house. Gabe smiled at how beautiful his wife looked. He kissed the top of her head lovingly.

"You two look so beautiful together, Gabriel," Ms. Mitchell told her son-in-law, watching him with her daughter.

"I was just thinking the same exact thing!" Ms. Jackson stated with a smile as she also sat and watched Shantae and Gabe.

"Nicole, are you ready to go?" Gabe asked his step-mother as he was gently shaking Shantae awake.

"We about to be out too, Momma!" Duke added as he and Melody stood up from the couch where the two were sitting.

As everyone was getting ready to leave, Gabe, Shantae, Duke, Melody, and Nicole all said their goodbyes as they headed outside.

"It better not be too long before I see y'all again!" Ms. Mitchell told Gabe and Shantae before she turned and repeated the same comment to Duke and Melody.

"You following me or heading home?" Gabe asked Shantae as the two of them stood up waiting until Nicole finished talking with Ms. Mitchell and Ms. Jackson.

"I'ma go home!" Shantae answered, just as Duke walked up.

"Gabe, what you about to do?"

"He's about to take his step-mom home, and then he's coming home too!" Shantae told her brother, answering for Gabe.

"Goddamn!" Duke said, shaking his head sadly.

"What up, bruh?" Gabe asked, seeing his brother-in-law's sudden change in facial expression.

Duke looked at Gabe and was still shaking his head.

"Damn, fam! I really think you done fucked up and married ya own prison warden, my dude!"

"Fuck you, nigga!" Shantae screamed, punching Duke in the chest as both he and Gabe burst out laughing.

"Naw, for real though!" Duke said, still lightly laughing but getting serious. "I was thinking, since we both retired from this street shit, I was thinking we could open up a business or something."

"Together?" Shantae asked her brother.

"Yeah!" Duke answered her.

"What type of business you talking about, playboy?" Gabe asked as Nicole walked up and stood next to Gabe.

"I was thinking we could open up a nightclub!" Duke announced. "But I'ma let you get Ms. Green home. I'll hit you up on your cell a little bit later tonight or tomorrow."

"Hit me up!" Gabe told his boy and then embraced him before his brother-in-law turned and walked off.

Gabe turned back to Shantae and kissed her, and then told her he would see her once he got back to the house.

"You ready?" he asked, looking at a smiling Nicole as she stood watching him.

"Yes, sweetheart!" she replied as she was escorted around to the passenger side of the Bentley.

Once Nicole was inside the car and Gabe walked around and got behind the wheel, he started up the Bentley and watched Shantae pull off and drive past him. He turned the Bentley around and drove off in the opposite direction and headed toward Nicole's house.

"I'm really happy and proud of you, Gabriel," Nicole told him, only to receive a smile from her step-son in return. "I really waited a long time to see you this happy."

"You helped me get here!" Gabe told her. "Thanks!"

"You don't have to thank me, Gabriel. I love you and only want you to be happy, sweetheart!"

"I am happy!"

"That's good!" she told him with big grin. "So, what's this I'm hearing about you and Duke wanting to open up a club?"

"It's one of Duke's newest ideas!" Gabe explained.

"How do you feel about it?" Nicole asked him. "I actually think it's a good idea considering you're both still young and know what the young people want to have and see to enjoy themselves."

"I actually like the idea!" Gabe admitted. "But I don't really know nothing about opening or running a club, Nicole."

"I may know someone that would be willing to help you if you're serious about this whole thing!" she informed him while smiling over at him.

Gabe looked at his step-mother after hearing her offer to help. He then focused back on the road.

"Nicole, I've noticed you don't ever question me about where I've gotten all my money or how I've been able to buy a Bentley or where I've been for a whole year. Why don't you?" he questioned.

Nicole gave up a little laugh at first while she stared out the window. She then turned back toward Gabe and met his gaze.

"Gabriel, I'm not blind or just stupid, sweetheart. And I'm not saying that you think I am either. I'm pretty sure you didn't win this money you have by chance; and truthfully, I really don't care to know how you obtain any of it. Because I see that you're trying to do something good with it. You've married that beautiful girl, so I'm just happy you're safe trying to become something!"

Gabe remained quiet after listening to Nicole and what she had to say concerning his lifestyle and well-being. He turned the Bentley down the street on which she lived and pulled in front of the house, just as his father was climbing out of his Mercedes.

"I guess I'll see you later, sweetheart," Nicole told him, leaning over to give Gabe a kiss on his cheek before he got out and walked around to open the door for her.

"Thank you, sweetheart!" Nicole said, smiling as she climbed out of the car. She then gave him a big hug. "I love you, Gabriel."

"I love you too—Mom!"

Nicole was shocked and frozen in surprise after what she had just heard Gabe call her. Nicole met his beautiful eyes as tears began to run down her face.

"Please call me when you get home, sweetheart, so I know you got home safe," Nicole told him.

She kissed Gabe on his cheek again before turning and entering the front yard. When she looked up, she saw her husband standing on the front porch with his face balled up and staring out at his son.

"What's wrong with you?" David asked his wife. "What the hell did that bas—?"

"Give it a rest, David!" Nicole told her husband, pushing past him as she entered the house.

David was surprised at his wife's attitude and her behavior. He looked back at the Bentley that was parked in front of his house to find his son standing at the open driver's door staring over at him. He then saw his son shake his head before he climbed back inside and pulled off a few moments later.

~ ~ ~

Gabe made it back to the condo a little while later after stopping for gas. He parked the Bentley beside Shantae's car and was climbing out when his cell phone went off from inside his pocket.

He sighed after pulling out the phone and seeing that Brianna was calling him, but he went ahead and answered the call anyway.

"Yeah, Brianna!"

"Gabe, you gotta be fucking joking! What the fuck is Erica talking about?"

"What are you talking about, Brianna?"

"Are you engaged to that bitch, Gabe?"

"No, Brianna!" Gabe told her, chuckling before he continued. "I'm married to the bitch you talking about!"

"What?" Brianna screamed. "Gabe, do not play the fuck with me! You did not marry that bitch!"

"Brianna, you know me well enough to know I don't play!" Gabe reminded her.

Gabe hit the locks on his car and looked up and saw Shantae and Duchess walking outside the condo. He returned his attention to the phone conversation he was having with Brianna, listening to her going off and yelling angrily at him.

"Who is that?" Shantae mouthed to Gabe.

"Brianna!" he replied after removing the phone from his mouth, only to have Shantae snatch it from his hand and hang up while Brianna was still yelling over the line.

"Relax, Shan!" Gabe told her, pulling his wife up against him as he wrapped his arms around her waist. He then gripped her ass cheeks in both of his hands. "She just found out about us getting married. Her sister told her!"

"How the hell does she know?"

"She had to see the ring when I met her earlier!"

"Excuse me, nigga!" Shantae exclaimed, pushing away from him. "Why am I just hearing about this visit? Why the hell you need to visit her anyway, Gabe?"

Gabe explained the visit with Erica to his wife, and let her know about the job offer that was made to him. Gabe saw the change in Shantae's face as she stood listening.

"What was your answer to this offer?" Shantae asked once Gabe was finished explaining to her.

"You really need to ask that, ma?" he asked as he then grabbed her and pulled her back up against him. "You know me well enough to know what my answer was."

"Well, you need to change your number!" Shantae told him just as Gabe's phone began to ring again.

She snatched it again and answered it this time, never looking to see who was calling.

"What?"

"Damn! You already screening my dude's calls?"

Shantae sucked her teeth after recognizing her brother's voice. She then handed Gabe his phone back.

"It's Duke's stupid ass!"

Gabe laughed lightly as he took the phone from her and placed it up to his ear.

"Yeah, fam! What's good?"

CHAPTER 13

After talking over the plan for a few days, Gabe and Duke came to an agreement about their new business idea, and they also let Boo Man in on the plans. Boo was the one who suggested adding a strip club to the nightclub idea, and he also became a partner. Gabe then brought up the idea of contacting their old school friend Simon, the computer genius.

Once the three of them were all in complete understanding and agreement on the plans, Gabe got in contact with his step-mother and explained to her the decisions that he, Duke, and Boo Man had made together. Nicole promised to contact her friend who would, in turn, get back in contact with the three young men. Gabe thanked her and then met up with Simon, who seemed happy to hear from him.

Gabe explained to Simon about wanting him to hook up the security system for the new nightclub and strip club they were going to be opening.

"Yes" was the quick and easy response Simon gave to Gabe.

After setting the plan in motion, Gabe, Duke, and Boo Man began looking around for a location for the nightclub and strip club. They let the girls help out, and they were in charge of going online to check out various locations and buildings.

Four days later, Gabe spoke in depth with his step-mother's friend Lisa Wells. She was a businesswoman who had managed a number of businesses as well as two clubs up in New York state.

Later in the day, Shantae, Melody, and Tamara then met with Gabe, Boo Man, and Duke and let them know about a location in a closed Super Walmart building that was located in Fort Lauderdale.

The group made the trip out to Fort Lauderdale, where they drove up and saw the huge warehouse building with the large, wide parking lot. The building was in a perfect spot, with a lot of traffic driving by throughout the day. Gabe looked at Duke and Boo Man, and both his boys' eyes were sparkling with great approval.

"I guess you two are feeling the spot as well, huh?" Gabe inquired with a big smirk on his face.

"Yo! Who's this?" Boo Man asked after seeing a Mercedes-Benz S-Class pulling up and heading in their direction slowly.

"Y'all relax!" Shantae spoke up, also seeing the S-Class. "That's the guy that's leasing the building to us. I called him on the way over here."

Gabe watched as the Benz parked and a dark-brown-skinned guy got out of the Benz. He was well dressed, with a clean-shaven head, which caused both Tamara and Melody to comment how handsome he looked.

"Mrs. Green?" he asked as he walked up to the group of six.

"Yes!" Shantae answered, getting his attention.

The man smiled once his eyes landed on Shantae.

He held out his hand to her and introduced himself: "I'm David Simmers."

"You'll be dealing with my husband, Mr. Simmers," Shantae informed him.

She then directed his attention over to a quiet and watchful Gabe, who stood leaning against the back of his Porsche with both arms folded across his chest. Gabe stood there with his normal dead-serious expression on his face.

"Mr. Green!" Mr. Simmers began after clearing his throat when he saw the look on Gabe's face.

Gabe ignored Simmers's hand and abruptly said,

"How about showing us the building, playboy!"

"Yes, sir!" Mr. Simmers answered, motioning the group to follow him across the expansive parking lot.

"Gabe, relax!" Shantae told her husband, seeing how tight he looked when he noticed how Mr. Simmers kept looking at his wife with the flirtatious smile he gave her. "Let's just get through this, okay?"

"Uh huh!" was Gabe's response as they all followed behind the leasing agent.

~ ~ ~

Two days after touring the building and deciding right there on the spot that they wanted it, Gabe met with his business manager and Nicole, who was now his new attorney. They then all met with David Simmers concerning the building.

Once all the paperwork was signed and completed and money was exchanged, Lisa Wells met with Gabe, Boo Man, and Duke. She explained to them everything that was necessary to get the building in order to get their business up and running.

Gabe then introduced his decision that he already had someone who was going to take care of half of the security as far as cameras, alarm systems, and other electronic issues were concerned. Gabe then informed Lisa to take care of whatever else was necessary to get the business going as soon as possible.

"That brings us to the issue of money!" Lisa said, looking at Gabe and then over at Duke and Boo Man. "I'm going to need money to take care of a lot of what needs to be done before you can open."

"This should help!" Gabe said as he dug out a Visa Platinum credit card. "Use that until I receive the business credit cards I've got coming."

"A man who's all about his business," Lisa said with a smile as she took the new platinum card with which to get to work.

~ ~ ~

Gabe, Duke, and Boo Man then met with Shantae, Melody, Tamara, and a few other girls and discussed the plans they had for the nightclub and strip club. Gabe explained to them that not only did they need girls for the strip club, but also as servers, bartenders, and dancers throughout the nightclub.

"So basically you want a whole female staff to work the club as well as females inside this strip club.

Is what you're saying, right?" Melody asked Gabe.

"Relax, shorty!" he told Melody. "I'm already looking into making sure the best security is working both clubs, so if anything does happen, it will be handled instantly without any of the girls having to worry."

"Shantae!" Boo Man spoke up. "How you feel about working with Tamara with taking care of the girls at the strip club?"

"I don't mind!" Shantae replied, looking over at a smiling Tamara.

"Melody, you with the team too, right?" Gabe asked her.

"What you want me to do?" she asked him.

"Since you're more of a people person, I want you working closely with Lisa. And since she's just the business manager, I'm making you the club's manager. You cool with that, Duke?" Gabe explained as he looked over at his brother-in-law.

"Yeah!" Duke answered, smiling as he stood staring at his wife as Melody stood smiling back at him. "I think that's a good idea, fam!"

~ ~ ~

Once construction began on the building, Gabe

made sure that he, Duke, and Boo Man had a part in getting the place put together. He even brought Simon into the building to allow him to get a look around and point out where he wanted the best video cameras placed out of view inside both of the clubs. Cameras were also going to be placed at the front and back entrances of both clubs, throughout the parking lot, and on the corners of the building.

After the new business credit cards had arrived, Gabe gave one to both Duke and Boo Man. He then gave Lisa a business card and took his personal card back from her.

While they were back overseeing some of the interior construction, Gabe received a call from Brianna. He took a moment and then answered.

"Yeah, Brianna!"

"Gabe, it's Sherry! We've got a problem!"

"What's up, Sherry?" Gabe replied with a sigh.

Gabe listened intently as Sherry explained that two of Brianna's spots had been raided by Miami PD, and also that she had received another message about doing business or being dealt with. Gabe admitted that he had completely forgotten about the problems Brianna was facing.

"Let me call you back, Sherry," Gabe told her.

After hanging up the phone, Gabe called the guy who Duke had introduced him to who was supposed to find out information on Peter Snow.

~ ~ ~

"What his ass say, Sherry?" Brianna asked as she sat across from her girl with Lorenzo after she hung up the phone.

"He said he's gonna call me back!" Sherry responded as she tossed Brianna's phone onto the coffee table.

"That's all he said?" Brianna asked with an attitude. "His ass probably laid up under that bitch he married!"

"Brianna, what we need to be doing until Gabe calls back is worrying about getting our workers out of jail!" Sherry told her girl just as the phone on the table went off.

Sherry picked it up and saw that it was Gabe calling her back.

"Yeah, Gabe!"

"Sherry, what was the officer's name who sent Brianna the first message after arresting Jit Jit?"

"I don't know his first name. Jit Jit never told us.

But it was Officer Jones," she told Gabe before she then asked, "What's going on, Gabe?"

"I'ma hit you up after I handle this bullshit!"

After hearing the line disconnect, Sherry looked at the screen and saw that Gabe had hung up again. She then looked over at Brianna and Lorenzo.

"He said he'll call me back again."

Brianna sucked her teeth as she angrily shot up out of her seat and left Sherry and Lorenzo in the den as she headed to her bedroom.

~ ~ ~

Gabe paid Gina a little money to go with him to Miami PD headquarters. He had her go inside to speak with Officer Jones; however, a female officer informed her that he was not there. Gina then asked her if she knew Jones's first name, and further explained that he was black and in his mid-thirties.

Gabe waited outside until Gina finally came back out to his car.

"What's up, cutie?" Gabe asked once Gina climbed inside.

"His name's Aaron Jones, and he's out in the field at the moment as the lady cop just said to me!" she answered.

"That's all you got from inside?" Gabe asked her.

She nodded her head yes and then added, "But I think I can find him."

"How?" Gabe questioned, watching Gina as she dug out her cell and began making phone calls.

Gabe started up the Porsche and then backed out of his parking spot and drove away from the police station. A few minutes after they were on the road, he picked up his Newports, just as Gina was hanging up the phone.

"Well, I called my girl Emily, and I've got some good news for you!" she said as she smiled over at Gabe.

"What up, cutie?" Gabe asked.

"Emily knows who this Jones officer is!" Gina informed Gabe. "I told her we're on our way over to talk to her now!"

"I got one question, Gina," Gabe told her. "Do you trust this chick?"

"Oh, I trust her, Gabe!" Gina responded to him. "She's proven that I can trust her. Believe me!"

~ ~ ~

Gabe met up with Gina's friend Emily and found out that ol' boy, Officer Aaron Jones, was actually a power head and was a regular customer of Emily's since she sold coke, weed, and some pills. Gabe then paid Emily $300 for her help and got her to contact Jones and see if she could get him to come over.

After Emily accepted the money and agreed to get Officer Jones over to the house, Gabe stepped outside, with Gina right behind him.

"Gabe, what are you about to do?" Gina asked him as she stood beside him on the front porch.

"Don't worry, cutie!" he said, looking over at her. "I won't have nothing I do fall back onto you or Emily."

Gabe and Gina heard the door open behind them as Emily stepped outside.

"He's on his way over now!" Emily announced as she stared straight at Gabe, who simply nodded his head in response.

~ ~ ~

Officer Jones arrived at Emily's house about ten minutes after receiving her call to come and see her. He pulled his squad car up in front of the house. When he stepped out of the car, he saw Emily walk outside with a smile on her face.

"What you got for me, baby?" Jones asked her as

he stepped up onto the porch and kissed Emily on the lips.

"Come on in, boo!" she told him, turning around and leading him into her house.

They spent less than five minutes inside as Emily served Jones a half ounce of coke after letting him try a little of what she was now selling. He gave Emily another kiss before he headed back out to his car, since he had to get to work.

He pulled off from Emily's place a few moments later with a smile on his face. He was feeling the effects of the good coke that he just hit before leaving her house.

"How's it going up there, Jones?"

"Holy shit!" Officer Jones yelled as he slammed on the brakes while trying to look back behind him.

"Who the fuck is you?" Jones yelled, staring into the back seat at the young guy who sat calmly staring back at him. "How the fuck you even get into my car?"

"I've got a few questions I wanna ask you!" Gabe began while completely ignoring the officer's questions.

Jones stared at the guy in his back seat as if he

were crazy. He then began shouting and went to open his door, but was swiftly grabbed around his throat by Gabe from the back with a gun pressed to the side of his head.

"You ready to talk or what?" Gabe asked in a whispered voice, speaking into Officer Jones's ear.

~ ~ ~

Gabe climbed out from the back seat of Officer Jones's car about twenty minutes later, now parked at an empty park. Gabe walked away from the squad car and headed out to the sidewalk just as his Porsche pulled up in front of him.

"You okay?" Gina asked once Gabe was inside the car.

"Yeah, I'm fine!" Gabe answered her as Gina was pulling off. "Go ahead and make the call now!"

Gina looked over at Gabe and realized what he was telling her. She dug out her cell phone and made the call to the police station reporting a possible murder of a police officer at Scott Lake Park.

Gabe barely listened to Gina; instead, he was thinking about what he had just found out and how he was going to handle things. He then pulled out his own cell phone and called Sherry's phone instead of

Brianna's.

"Hello!"

"Sherry, this is Gabe."

"Gabe, what's up? What happened?"

"Just let Brianna know I'ma deal with her little issue, so she can relax."

"I'll let her know. You alright though? You sound a little different—like something's wrong!"

"I'm good!" Gabe told her. "Call if you need me."

~ ~ ~

Sherry hung up with Gabe but was still confused at how odd his voice sounded. She then made a call to Brianna as she was slowing to a stop at a red light.

"Hello!"

"I just spoke with Gabe," Sherry said, ignoring Brianna's attitude.

"And?"

"And he says that you can relax!" she told her girl, explaining to Brianna what Gabe had told her to tell her.

Brianna remained quiet a few moments and then spoke up: "Why didn't he call me and tell me all that himself?"

"Brianna, we not about to play games!" Sherry told her as she pulled off after the light turned green. "What we need to worry about now is getting our guys out of jail and letting Gabe handle what he's there to handle."

CHAPTER 14

Three days after receiving the call from Sherry giving her the message from Gabe that he would handle the problem with which she was dealing, Brianna first heard the news report on the murder of Officer Aaron Jones. The police labeled the death as a drug-related murder, since the officer was found shot in the head with an ounce of cocaine in his possession.

Two days after the report on Officer Jones's murder, Brianna then heard from Sherry and Lorenzo, who told her the latest news. It was at that time that she learned the story of the murder of Peter Snowhite, also known as Peter Snow. The report stated that Mr. Snow had connections to Officer Jones as well as a few other officers and detectives who were now under investigation.

Brianna heard her phone ring as soon as she hung up with Sherry and Lorenzo. She was surprised to see that it was Gabe on the line.

"Hello!"

"Brianna, it's Gabe!"

"I know!"

"You seen the news yet?"

"No! But I've heard from Sherry the good news. Thank you!"

"Everything should be cool from here on out! I'ma make sure of it, but if you need me, let me know."

"I do need you, Gabe! Baby, I love and miss you so much!"

"Bye, Brianna!"

Brianna then suddenly heard the line die while she was still confessing her love for him. She looked down at her phone and saw that Gabe had hung up again. She felt tears as they began running down her face, but she also began to feel anger and something new and much stronger: hate.

~ ~ ~

Gabe grabbed his phone and called another number after hanging up with Brianna. He sat listening to the line ring until it was finally answered.

"Hello!"

"Erica, it's Gabe!"

"I'm aware of that, Gabe! What can I do for you today?"

"I'll make this real short, Erica," he told her. "I

know about you and Peter Snow. We won't get into it, but you know how I know since you saw the news, and I'm pretty sure you know who's responsible for what happened. I'm saying this only once. Leave her alone, or the next time I call you is to let you know I'm coming to visit you!"

Gabe hung up the phone before Erica could attempt to say anything else. He then looked back at his cell phone screen once it began ringing in his hand.

"Yeah, Lisa!" Gabe answered after seeing that it was his new business manager calling.

He looked up to see Shantae and Tamara walking in the front door as he sat down at the breakfast bar.

"I've got some good news, Gabe!" he heard Lisa begin to say just as Shantae beat her to it and announced that the building was finished and both the nightclub and strip club were almost ready.

"Lisa, you a few seconds too late!" Gabe told her with a smile as Shantae leaned in and kissed him on the lips.

~ ~ ~

"Hello!"

"Mr. Galileo, we've got a problem . . . It's

Gabriel!" Erica said as she began explaining the phone call that she had just received a few minutes ago.

"Okay!" Mr. Galileo replied with a deep sigh. "So this young man knows what we were up to, but do you think you can still convince him to come and work for me?"

Erica remained quiet a few moments and considered the question that he just asked her. She was honest when she answered.

"Truthfully, I do not know! After Gabriel broke up with my sister I thought I could control him better. However, it's not working out like I thought it would!"

"Maybe I need to pay him a visit and speak with him one-on-one."

"No!" Erica cried. "Let me try one more thing! I think I can convince him if I can talk to him face-to-face! Let me work one more try on him."

"Do what you must!" Mr. Galileo told her. "If your way does not work this time, I will see to Mr. Green my own way!"

~ ~ ~

Gabe arrived at the newly renovated building that

was soon to be the new nightclub and strip club. He got out of the back of Tamara's new 2018-model BMW X1 that Boo Man had gifted her, just as Shantae was climbing out of the front passenger seat. Gabe then dropped his arm around her shoulders as the three of them started walking toward the front entrance of the massive building.

Gabe allowed Shantae to unlock the club's front door. The place seemed even wider and was converted into a two-story building, with the nightclub on the bottom floor and the strip club on the top level. Gabe then followed his wife and Tamara into the dark building.

"Let me hit the lights!" Tamara said as she walked off.

"So you've seen the place already?" Gabe asked Shantae.

"I sure did!" she answered, just as all the lights began coming on.

She turned around and saw Gabe with an actual smile on his face, and then she saw his dimples that he rarely allowed to fully show.

"This is what I'm talking about!" Gabe stated as he began walking around and looking at all the renovations to the building.

He loved the wide stage and nodded in approval at the four platforms in all four corners of the club. He also liked the square glass booth that was in the dead center of the club, which had enough room for two dancers with a stripper pole.

"You wanna look upstairs?" Shantae asked Gabe as she took his hand and began leading him toward the glass elevator on the right side of the club. There was a matching twin glass elevator on the far-left side as well.

After they stepped off the elevator once the doors opened on the second level, Shantae escorted Gabe and showed him around. The two of them walked through the tunnel-like hallway that was made mostly of glass, which allowed a perfect view of the dance floor and most of the club's first level.

"What do you think?" Shantae asked Gabe as the two of them entered into one of four VIP rooms that each resembled a mini version of the downstairs nightclub. They were each set up with a dance floor and surrounded by three house-style booths and their own bar.

Gabe nodded his head in approval with a smile

on his lips. He opened his mouth to speak, when he suddenly heard his name being called from inside the building. He looked over at Shantae, who also had a questioning expression on her face.

The two of them then walked over to the gold-plated rail and looked down through the glass onto the first level. Gabe and Shantae then saw Boo Man and Duke with Tamara looking up at them. Shantae waved them to come up and then turned back toward her husband with a big smile.

"You know I love you, right?" Shantae asked while locking her hands behind his neck.

Gabe then took possession of her ass, gripping both cheeks in his hands right before he kissed her directly on the lips.

"You two find a room for all that shit!" Duke joked as he, Boo Man, and Tamara entered the VIP room.

Gabe embraced Duke and Boo Man after releasing Shantae. He then did a 360-degree look around the strip club.

"We almost finished, my niggas! The hard part is over; now we gotta get started on getting business up and running!"

"Fam, what do you think we been doing all this time?" Duke asked him. "You ain't the only one handling business. Me and Boo Man already put in work getting security put together for both the clubs."

"We already started getting the big guys together!" Tamara continued telling Gabe. "They had to take an AIDS test and a test for any other type of nasty-ass shit their asses could be carrying."

"We just waiting on you now!" Shantae said, drawing Gabe's attention over to her. "Hey, and what's up with these security cameras you keep talking about that you have to put in the building?"

Gabe smiled as he stared at his wife. He dug into his pocket, pulled out his cell phone, and pulled up Simon's number to call the boy genius.

Shantae shook her head and smiled at Gabe. She then looked over at Tamara and saw her girl also smiling and watching Gabe. For some reason, Shantae didn't feel the need to say something to Tamara to defend who Gabe was to her.

"A'ight, you all happy now?" Gabe announced, drawing Shantae's attention back over to him. "I just got at my boy about getting things set up, and he's on his way out here right now to get started."

"Who is this person you keep talking about?" Shantae asked him.

Gabe smiled and said, "You remember Simon from school?"

"Simon?" Shantae repeated. "You talking about the smart muthafucker that messes with computers, Gabe?"

Gabe nodded in agreement and still had a big grin on his face.

"He's the only one I trust to set this system up for us. I know he knows what the fuck he's doing since we've dealt with him before."

"We?" Shantae inquired.

"Let's just say Simon had a big part to play with me, Boo Man, and Duke being where we are at now and able to do what we are doing now!" Gabe admitted to Shantae, giving her a quick wink.

CHAPTER 15

S hantae was surprised at how packed the nightclub, Club 301, was on its opening night. She nodded her head at a few people she knew or recognized. She then made her way through the crowd with her personal bodyguard assigned to her by Gabe. She stopped behind her bodyguard as he opened a door marked "Owners Only."

She took the executive elevator up to the second-floor level and then followed her bodyguard once they stepped off. Shantae headed up the hallway and stopped at the owners' office, knocking once before entering.

"Gimme just a minute, Bear!" Shantae informed her bodyguard before shutting the office door.

Shantae turned around to face Duke, who sat behind his desk talking on his desk phone. She looked over at her husband's desk across the large and spacious office. She walked over and sat down in the tall, black-leather office chair behind the dark cherry-wood desk.

Shantae picked up the desk phone and made a call to Gabe.

"Yeah, Shantae?" Gabe answered at the start of the second ring.

"How'd you know it was me?" she asked him, but she never gave him the chance to answer. "Where the hell are you, boy? You do remember you have both Trey Songz and Rick Ross performing here tonight at the club's opening, right?"

"Shan, relax!" Gabe told her with a chuckle.

"Nigga, is you fucking—?"

"Shantae!" Gabe said, raising his voice and cutting her off. "You're on the speaker phone, and Nicole is in the car with me."

"Why didn't you tell me I was on the speaker phone, boy?" Shantae said before she apologized to Gabe's step-mother.

"It's okay, Shantae!" Nicole called out.

"Shan, relax!" Gabe repeated again. "I'm on my way. But if Ross and Trey Songz arrive before I do, remember that Duke also owns part of the club too, right?"

Shantae lifted her eyes and looked over to Duke, who was standing at the dark-tinted, thick window that allowed a full view of the entire club. She asked Gabe how long it would be before he arrived at the club.

"Soon!" was Gabe's answer before he hung up the phone.

Shantae sucked her teeth after the phone died. She hung up the headset and walked over to stand beside Duke and look over the club.

"You don't trust me now?" Duke questioned his sister after a few silent moments. He then looked over at her and continued, "You do remember I'm also part owner of this place too, right?"

"Boy, I ain't forget!" Shantae admitted. "I just want Gabe where I am. I haven't really spent any time with him these last three months since he's been dealing with getting this place together with you, Boo Man, and Lisa. I want my man with me!"

Duke smiled after listening to his sister. He then wrapped his arm around her shoulder and hugged her. He started to say something, when there was a knock at the office door.

"Who is it?" Shantae called out, when the door suddenly opened and Bear allowed Lisa inside.

"Where's Gabriel at? Is he here yet?" Lisa asked as she looked around for him in the office.

Duke shook his head and smiled.

LOYALTY TO A GANGSTA 2

"Gabe isn't here yet, Lisa. What can I help you with?" he asked.

Lisa paused for a moment after remembering that Duke was also an owner. She had been mostly dealing with Gabe.

"Trey Songz has just arrived. I have him up in the owners' box waiting to see either you or Gabe."

"Rick Ross still hasn't made it here yet?" Shantae asked the business manager.

"I've spoken with Mr. Ross's manager and was informed that they would be here within the next thirty minutes," Lisa answered while looking over at Duke, who was at his desk gathering up papers.

"Okay, let's go!" Duke stated after getting the papers he needed and heading for the door.

~ ~ ~

"Oh my God!" Nicole cried out once Gabe pulled the Bentley up in front of the new nightclub he and his friends owned. "Gabriel, look at how crowded it is!"

Gabe smiled when he saw all the cars, trucks, and SUVs filling the parking lot. He even peeped the huge line that was forming outside the front door of Club 301 and Club Shock, which was the strip club that Boo Man ran. Gabe pulled the Bentley up to the door, and all eyes were on his car.

Gabe climbed out of his car as the passenger door was opened by security for Nicole. He left the keys inside the Bentley as young Derrick rushed around to park the car.

"What's up, boss man?" Derrick called out before jumping into the Bentley.

Gabe shook his head as Derrick pulled off in his car. He then turned back to his step-mother just as the head of security walked out of the club.

"Silk, what's up?" Gabe asked, dapping up with the boy as Nicole wrapped her hand around his arm.

"What up, Gabe?" Silk answered, and then smiled when he saw Nicole. "Mrs. Green, it's good seeing you again. But I'm beginning to get jealous now after seeing how gorgeous you look tonight, knowing I can't take you home afterward."

"Alright now!" Gabe said as Nicole giggled after listening to Silk.

"Duke's up with Lisa talking with Trey Songz and his manager," Silk informed Gabe as the three of them entered the club.

Once they were inside the club, Gabe found out

from Silk where Lisa and Duke were, and then had Silk take Nicole up to the VIP room with other friends and family members who came to tonight's opening.

After Silk escorted Nicole off, Gabe made his way up to the owners' box where he was told Lisa and Duke were meeting with Trey.

Gabe entered the room and was immediately introduced by Lisa by name and title. He then shook hands with the manager and dapped up with a surprisingly cool-as-hell Trey Songz. Gabe kicked it for a few minutes with the R&B star and then gave the guy some alone time to get right. Gabe then followed Lisa and Duke out of the owners' box and saw his wife leaning against the wall dressed in a cream-white Dolce & Gabbana pantsuit.

"Hey, you!" Shantae said, smiling at the sight of her husband. She looked him over in his silk gray and cream-white Armani suit and matching suede Armani loafers.

"What's up, ma?" Gabe said, smiling as he grabbed her around the waist. He pulled her up against him, only to grip her ass before kissing her.

"I miss you too!" Shantae said after the kiss

ended, now with an even bigger smile on her face.

"I'm impressed though!" Gabe stated as he peeped back and looked down at the stiletto heels she was wearing. "You actually wearing heels and not ya Tims?"

"They're inside my office with a change of clothes," Shantae said, causing Gabe to burst out laughing.

Gabe left the owners' box and made his way around to the office, where he found Duke and Lisa already inside having a conversation. Gabe left Shantae at the door talking with Bear, her bodyguard.

"So, what's up with Ross? Is he here yet?" Gabe asked with a sigh as he fell into his desk chair.

"He and his manager should be here in fifteen minutes," Lisa replied.

Lisa then began repeating the information that she had just received from Melody concerning someone named Murphy renting one of the VIP booths for the night.

"You say who?" Gabe asked, instantly recognizing the name.

"It was Murphy!" Lisa replied to her boss.

"Gabe, what's wrong?" Shantae asked her

husband when she quickly noticed his facial expression as she started toward his desk.

He slowly shook his head thinking Lisa couldn't possibly be talking about the guy he was thinking it was. He then allowed Shantae to sit on his lap as he answered her question.

"It's nothing, ma! I'm just tripping."

~ ~ ~

Gabe made an appearance upstairs and checked out the strip club. He wanted to make sure everything was running okay. He then kicked it with Tamara for a few minutes. He found his way over to the main floor of the strip club, and he saw that it was just as packed as the nightclub was downstairs.

Gabe was greeted at the entrance to the strip club by the beautiful hostess who was placed there by Shantae. He declined the escort that was offered, and decided to walk around by himself and get a look around. He actually liked the setup of how Boo Man, Shantae, and Tamara had the club looking. He was stopped by different girls that danced at the club and seemed happy to see him.

"Enjoying yourself too much, huh?" Gabe heard a voice behind him.

He looked over his shoulder and wasn't surprised to see Shantae right behind him. He smiled as he turned to face his wife.

"Let me find out you jealous, ma!" Gabe told her, brushing her hair back out of her face with his finger. "Finish showing me around."

"You probably seen enough already!" Shantae told him, rolling her eyes at Gabe as she started to walk off.

Gabe followed behind her as she supposedly was showing him around the club. But Gabe could barely pay any attention to his surroundings since he was too focused on the sway of Shantae's hips and the bounce of her ass as she sashayed her way through the club in front of him.

Gabe grabbed her as soon as the two of them entered the door marked for the owner, and he pushed her against the wall. He was pressed up against his wife kissing her on the lips, only for Shantae to respond with the same hunger and need.

"Wait!" Shantae moaned, breaking their breathless kiss. She gently pushed against Gabe's chest even though she really wanted to pull him hard against her.

"What's up?" Gabe asked in confusion while staring at Shantae.

"Not here!" she told him as she straightened out her pantsuit. She then took a deep breath and released it loudly, trying to calm herself. "I want your ass too, but this isn't the place for that!"

Gabe nodded his head in agreement. He then smiled and kissed Shantae's lips and said, "You know I love you, right?"

"I know!" Shantae replied as she smiled and began walking up the dimly lit hallway with a smiling Gabe right behind her.

They made it to Boo Man's private office and knocked on the door. They heard him call out from inside to come in. Shantae then opened the door and entered his office first, followed by Gabe.

"My dude!" Boo Man happily cried out, hopping up from his desk chair after seeing Gabe walk into his office.

Gabe was impressed with the suit Boo Man was wearing, and he embraced his big homie after Boo rushed him and gave him a bear hug. Gabe got away from him as both Shantae and Tamara stood off to the side laughing.

"It's looking good in here, fam!" Gabe told Boo Man as he looked around the office that was smaller than his and Duke's office, but was hooked up just as nicely.

"Bruh, business is just crazy good!" Boo Man replied, smiling hard. "With all these gorgeous girls Shantae and Tamara got in here, the niggas parked up in here and upstairs are going stupid over them. I ain't even mentioned the chicks that are up in this bitch nightclub too, bruh!"

"And that's how we gotta keep it!" Gabe told him just as the knocking started at the office door.

"Yeah!" Boo Man called out, only for the office door to open as Bear and Tamara's personal bodyguard, Tank, entered.

"What's up, Bear?" Shantae asked her bodyguard.

Bear looked at Gabe and then said, "Gabe, Silk just called me on the radio. He needs you at the front door!"

Moving before the last word left Bear's lips, Gabe shot out of the office door unaware of Shantae, Boo Man, and Tamara right behind him.

~ ~ ~

Silk saw the front doors to Club Shock fly open and Gabe rush out of the strip club. Silk called to his boy and waved him over as he stood facing the older gentleman and the familiar-looking female with their team of security.

"Mr. Green!" Mr. Galileo greeted after noticing Gabe walking through the doors that led to the upstairs strip club. "It's good to see you again."

"What the hell are the two of you doing here?" Gabe asked as he looked first at Mr. Galileo and then over to Erica.

Security instantly crowded around him as he faced the Italian and Erica.

"Gabe, we're just here to talk to you about—!"

"Talk about what?" Shantae spoke up as she and Tamara pushed through security to stand at Gabe's side.

"Who's your friend, Mr. Green?" Mr. Galileo asked, looking over the extremely attractive young woman.

"His friend is really his wife!" Shantae corrected the Italian. "How about announcing who the fuck you and the bitch with you are!"

"Mr. Green!" Mr. Galileo stated while looking

back at Gabe. "How about you and I talk like men, and you can dismiss the young woman beside you?"

"Shan!" Gabe spoke up before she had a chance to go the fuck off. "Mr. Galileo, I tell you what. Since Erica doesn't seem to have given you my answer from the last time you sent her to talk to me, I'm here to tell you myself that I'm not interested in anything you have to offer. And make this the last time that I have to see either one of you, because I'm getting really tired of seeing you both. Now please leave my place of business or be escorted the fuck off! Which do you prefer?"

Gabe held the Italian man's eyes for a moment and saw the look on his face that he tried to hide. Gabe then simply ignored the smile that Galileo gave him before he turned and began to walk away.

"Gabe, I really don't think—!"

"I think you need to follow the old man," Shantae ordered Erica while cutting her off.

Erica stared at Gabe's wife and then looked at Gabe and met his eyes. She shook her head as she turned and walked off.

~ ~ ~

"Mr. Galileo, I'm really sorry!" Erica told the

drug lord after the two of them were inside the back of the limousine in which they arrived. She opened her mouth to continue, only for Mr. Galileo to hold up his hand for her to shut up.

"I am finished with dealing with this friend of yours!" he stated as he picked up his car phone and made a call.

Erica could only shake her head as she turned her attention out the window. She sat wondering what she could possibly do to fix what was happening, when she heard him mention having someone dealt with. She looked over at the drug lord and listened as Mr. Galileo requested that Antonio and Manny be sent to Miami.

"Mr. Galileo!" Erica said once he hung up the phone. "Are you about to do what I think you are?"

He ignored the question that she had asked.

"We will be changing our plans as of this moment. We will no longer go through those you've mentioned. I've decided that I will handle things my way from here on out!"

"I really don't think that's—!"

"Contact your father and set up a meeting for us to get together!" Mr. Galileo ordered, cutting Erica off in the middle of what she was saying. "He either wants to work together as a business associate, or he can go out of business. Set the meeting up!"

Erica shook her head and was beginning to regret her decision to deal with Mr. Galileo after choosing to go against her own father because she felt he overlooked her and favored Brianna. She sighed deeply since she was quite unsure what exactly she was going to do now.

~ ~ ~

"Who was that, Gabe?" Shantae asked as soon as she, Gabe, Tamara, Silk, and Boo Man were all inside Gabe and Duke's office after the situation with Mr. Galileo and Erica had come to an end.

"Shan, just relax for a—!"

"Gabe, if you tell me to relax right now, I promise we will have a real problem in this office tonight!" Shantae told him, cutting off his comment.

"Shantae!" Tamara spoke up, seeing the look on Gabe's face at the very moment. She then stepped up beside Shantae. "That was Erica, Shantae! Brianna's step-sister!"

"What the fuck she doing here?" Shantae asked while still staring at Gabe. "And who the fuck was that white dude with that bitch?"

Gabe sat back in his desk chair and folded his hands across his mid-section. He calmly answered his wife. "His name is Galileo. He's some Italian dude who Erica's fucking with that's supposed to help her take over her father's business."

"Gabe, wait!" Tamara spoke up, now with a worried expression on her face. "You said Erica's working with this guy to do what with him?"

Gabe explained what he knew and admitted that he never mentioned anything to Darrell about what he knew, since he worked for himself and no longer had any dealings with Darrell. However, Gabe was unable to finish what he was saying when Tamara interrupted him.

"Gabe, you've got to help Darrell!" she cried out. "Don't you realize that if this guy goes up against Darrell and anything happens, it can mean something might happen to Brianna as well!"

"What the fuck does that have to do with Gabe?" Shantae asked with a great deal of attitude.

"Shantae, it's not like that!" Tamara stated, and was just about to continue when Gabe spoke up.

"Tamara, my word was made to protect Brianna,

not Darrell or his business!" he explained. "If Brianna needs me, I'll be there; but until then, I'ma do exactly what I'm doing—taking care of my family!"

Gabe stood up and stepped from behind his desk and headed straight for the door. He listened to Shantae's heels clicking on the tile as she followed behind him. He opened the door and then stepped to the side allowing her to walk out of the office first. He then followed her out and shut the door behind him.

Gabe and Shantae quietly walked together with Bear a few feet behind them. The two were in deep thought about their own issues until Shantae broke the silence.

"We need to talk about his whole thing with you and Brianna!"

Gabe sighed as the two of them approached the VIP booth where family and friends were seated, and he simply said, "Shan, just trust me. Please!"

CHAPTER 16

Three days after the opening of the club, Shantae was still feeling a certain way about the news she found out concerning her husband and his ex-girlfriend, even after Gabe had explained it to her.

Shantae was on her way to meet up with Tamara, who had wanted to meet up and have a conversation. Shantae dug out her phone as it began ringing. She checked the screen and saw that it was Gabe.

"What, Gabe?"

"Shan, where you at?"

"I already told you before I left the condo this morning that I was going to meet up with Tamara!"

Gabe sighed loudly into the phone before he began explaining that the two of them needed to talk. He then informed Shantae that he wanted her to meet him at Granny B's Soul Kitchen in two hours.

Shantae pulled her Lexus LS500 to a stop at the traffic light. She listened until Gabe had finished talking before she said what she had to say.

"Gabe, if we're meeting to talk about this bull—!" she paused in mid-sentence when she saw a movement to her left outside her window.

Shantae instantly swung her head to the left.

"Shit!" she yelled just as the driver's window exploded.

She pushed her seat back just barely in time before a bullet slammed into her face by the would-be assassin. She threw the driver's door open with force, catching the assassin by surprise as the door slammed hard into his mid-section and sent him tumbling backward.

She was out of the car within seconds with her Glock out and taking aim, and she let it speak loudly.

Boom! Boom! Boom! Boom!

After she opened up the killer's chest and face, Shantae stood over the body just as she heard another shot fired. Seconds later, pain exploded from her upper left arm and sent her to the ground hard.

She scrambled around to the front end of the Lexus while shots were still being taken at her. She looked at the blood that covered her left arm as the pain began to increase.

"I can't believe this shit!" Shantae growled as she then peeked around the side of the front of the Lexus.

Boom! Boom!

"Shit!" Shantae screamed after ducking back out

of the way from multiple shots that were being fired at her.

Doing some quick thinking while hearing the police in the distance, Shantae got flat onto her chest, looked under the car, and could see the second shooter a few feet away from the first one. She could see that he was on a cell phone yet still gripping the chrome piece he was using to shoot at her.

Boom! Boom! Boom!

Shantae let her Glock speak again, shooting from under the Lexus and watching the would-be killer drop to the ground screaming in pain and reaching for his leg and knees that were blown out. Shantae quickly got to her feet and made her way over to the second killer. She met his eyes once he looked up at her and smiled.

"Who the fuck is you?" Shantae asked, ignoring the smile on his face. "What the hell the two of you want?"

"You're dead!"

"Naw!" Shantae said as she raised her Glock and aimed straight for his face. "But you is though!"

Boom! Boom!

~ ~ ~

Gabe was inside his Porsche and on the phone calling Duke and the rest of the crew after hanging up with Tamara after what the hell he heard while he was on the phone talking with Shantae. He was speeding in the direction Tamara told him she and Shantae were meeting.

Gabe saw the road blocked off and the crowd of onlookers and police officers everywhere. He instantly spotted Tamara's ride just as he heard his cell phone begin ringing in his lap.

"Yeah!" Gabe answered the phone without checking the caller ID.

"Gabe, it's Tamara."

"Where you at?" he asked her. "I'm out here on 47th. I see ya ride out here, but I don't see you."

Gabe listened to Tamara explain that she was with Shantae after finding her shot and bleeding in the middle of the road. She then told him that she was on her way to take Shantae to see a friend who was a private-practice doctor.

Gabe interrupted Tamara and asked her for the address of the doctor.

After hanging up the phone after getting the information he requested, Gabe floored the Porsche, flew away from the scene, and headed in the direction to find his wife. His anger was at a new level.

"Somebody's gonna die!" Gabe mumbled as he gripped the steering wheel tighter.

~ ~ ~

The sudden banging caught Shantae and Dr. Lowell by surprise. Tamara met Shantae's eyes as she slowly shook her head and gave a small smile.

"He's gonna go stupid, Shantae!" Tamara told her as the banging started back up, which caused Dr. Lowell to jump again.

"Who is that pounding so hard at my front door, Tamara?" Dr. Lowell asked while staring at her.

"Her husband!" Tamara answered, shaking her head as she then turned and headed out to the front door.

"You're married, young lady?" Dr. Lowell asked as he continued stitching up Shantae's arm.

She opened her mouth to answer, when she heard Tamara cry out to Gabe. Shantae then swung her head around toward the room door after it flew open and smashed into the wall. She lay there staring at her husband's eyes—and the murderous look in them.

"Gabe, I'm—!"

"Who did this?" Gabe asked in a voice that was just above a whisper. But it came out like a growl and caused the doctor to look up from his work and stare at Gabe.

Shantae shook her head and said, "Babe, I don't know! It was two guys with an out-of-town type of accent."

"How they look?" he asked her.

"Tamara!" Shantae said, nodding for her to give Gabe her cell phone.

"What's this?" Gabe asked as Tamara handed him the touchscreen.

"I took pictures of the two guys who tried to kill me!" Shantae told Gabe. "You may not be able to see too much of the first one's face, since I tried to erase the shit!"

Gabe looked at the four pictures of the two supposed hit men. He then simply turned and walked out of the room and dug out his cell phone.

"Go with him, Tamara," Shantae said as she watched him leave.

"What about—?"

"I'll call Duke and Boo Man to come get me,"

Shantae said, cutting her girl off. "Go with Gabe!"

~ ~ ~

Gabe was inside the Porsche and starting up the car as the passenger door was snatched open. He had his new Taurus 9mm out and aimed at Tamara just as her ass touched the seat.

"Whoa!" Tamara cried out, pushing the gun out of her face. "It's just me!"

"Where you going?" Gabe asked as he set the 9 back down into his lap.

"Shantae wants me to go with you!" Tamara told him. "So don't say anything else. Duke, Boo Man, and Silk are on their way over to get her, so let's go!"

Gabe didn't bother going back and forth with Tamara. He simply threw the Porsche into first and pulled off from in front of the private clinic. He was already in third gear and flying up the street.

"So, where we going?" Tamara asked after a short while, looking over to see the look on Gabe's extremely handsome face.

"I'ma get some answers!" Gabe replied as he floored the Porsche, ignoring traffic and the threat of drawing the attention of the police.

~ ~ ~

Erica grabbed her purse from the couch and then picked up her keys and cell phone from the coffee table. She left the den and started toward the front door, when her cell phone began ringing in her hand.

"Hey there, Daddy!" Erica answered after seeing her father's name appear on the phone's screen.

She unlocked her front door and stepped out into the hallway of her building.

"Where are you, Erica? You were supposed to be here thirty minutes ago."

"Daddy, I had to take—!" she paused in the middle of her explanation to her father while she was standing in front of the elevator, just as the doors slid open.

She then found herself staring into the cold and deadly eyes of Gabe.

"What are you—?"

"Who are these two?" Gabe asked as he held up Shantae's cell phone and showed her the pictures of the two would-be hit men.

Erica stared at the touchscreen after taking the phone from Gabe. She looked at all four pictures and recognized one of the two bodies, since she could not make out the other man who was missing most of his face. She then looked up to meet those same hard eyes.

"Gabe, I promise I had nothing—!"

"Where is he?" Gabe demanded, cutting Erica off

in the middle of what she was saying. "This muthafucker tried to kill my wife. Now I'ma kill his ass! No trying to save him, because the muthafucker is gonna die! Where the fuck is he, Erica?"

Erica slowly shook her head after listening to what she was just told by Gabe. She sighed as she turned and started back toward her front door.

"We gotta talk, Gabe!"

Text Good2Go at 31996 to receive new release updates via text message.

Item Name	Price	Qty	Amount
48 Hours to Die – Silk White	$14.99		
A Hustler's Dream - Ernest Morris	$14.99		
A Hustler's Dream 2 - Ernest Morris	$14.99		
A Thug's Devotion – J. L. Rose and J. M. McMillon	$14.99		
Black Reign – Ernest Morris	$14.99		
Bloody Mayhem Down South – Trayvon Jackson	$14.99		
Bloody Mayhem Down South 2 – Trayvon Jackson	$14.99		
Business Is Business – Silk White	$14.99		
Business Is Business 2 – Silk White	$14.99		
Business Is Business 3 – Silk White	$14.99		
Childhood Sweethearts – Jacob Spears	$14.99		
Childhood Sweethearts 2 – Jacob Spears	$14.99		
Childhood Sweethearts 3 - Jacob Spears	$14.99		
Childhood Sweethearts 4 - Jacob Spears	$14.99		
Connected To The Plug – Dwan Marquis Williams	$14.99		
Connected To The Plug 2 – Dwan Marquis Williams	$14.99		
Connected To The Plug 3 – Dwan Williams	$14.99		
Deadly Reunion – Ernest Morris	$14.99		
Dream's Life – Assa Raymond Baker	$14.99		
Flipping Numbers – Ernest Morris	$14.99		
Flipping Numbers 2 – Ernest Morris	$14.99		
He Loves Me, He Loves You Not - Mychea	$14.99		
He Loves Me, He Loves You Not 2 - Mychea	$14.99		
He Loves Me, He Loves You Not 3 - Mychea	$14.99		
He Loves Me, He Loves You Not 4 – Mychea	$14.99		

He Loves Me, He Loves You Not 5 – Mychea	$14.99		
Lord of My Land – Jay Morrison	$14.99		
Lost and Turned Out – Ernest Morris	$14.99		
Married To Da Streets – Silk White	$14.99		
M.E.R.C. - Make Every Rep Count Health and Fitness	$14.99		
Money Make Me Cum – Ernest Morris	$14.99		
My Besties – Asia Hill	$14.99		
My Besties 2 – Asia Hill	$14.99		
My Besties 3 – Asia Hill	$14.99		
My Besties 4 – Asia Hill	$14.99		
My Boyfriend's Wife - Mychea	$14.99		
My Boyfriend's Wife 2 – Mychea	$14.99		
My Brothers Envy – J. L. Rose	$14.99		
My Brothers Envy 2 – J. L. Rose	$14.99		
Naughty Housewives – Ernest Morris	$14.99		
Naughty Housewives 2 – Ernest Morris	$14.99		
Naughty Housewives 3 – Ernest Morris	$14.99		
Naughty Housewives 4 – Ernest Morris	$14.99		
Never Be The Same – Silk White	$14.99		
Shades of Revenge – Assa Raymond Baker	$14.99		
Slumped – Jason Brent	$14.99		
Someone's Gonna Get It – Mychea	$14.99		
Stranded – Silk White	$14.99		
Supreme & Justice – Ernest Morris	$14.99		
Supreme & Justice 2 – Ernest Morris	$14.99		
Supreme & Justice 3 – Ernest Morris	$14.99		
Tears of a Hustler - Silk White	$14.99		
Tears of a Hustler 2 - Silk White	$14.99		
Tears of a Hustler 3 - Silk White	$14.99		
Tears of a Hustler 4- Silk White	$14.99		
Tears of a Hustler 5 – Silk White	$14.99		
Tears of a Hustler 6 – Silk White	$14.99		
The Panty Ripper - Reality Way	$14.99		
The Panty Ripper 3 – Reality Way	$14.99		

The Solution – Jay Morrison	$14.99		
The Teflon Queen – Silk White	$14.99		
The Teflon Queen 2 – Silk White	$14.99		
The Teflon Queen 3 – Silk White	$14.99		
The Teflon Queen 4 – Silk White	$14.99		
The Teflon Queen 5 – Silk White	$14.99		
The Teflon Queen 6 - Silk White	$14.99		
The Vacation – Silk White	$14.99		
Tied To A Boss - J.L. Rose	$14.99		
Tied To A Boss 2 - J.L. Rose	$14.99		
Tied To A Boss 3 - J.L. Rose	$14.99		
Tied To A Boss 4 - J.L. Rose	$14.99		
Tied To A Boss 5 - J.L. Rose	$14.99		
Time Is Money - Silk White	$14.99		
Tomorrow's Not Promised – Robert Torres	$14.99		
Tomorrow's Not Promised 2 – Robert Torres	$14.99		
Two Mask One Heart – Jacob Spears and Trayvon Jackson	$14.99		
Two Mask One Heart 2 – Jacob Spears and Trayvon Jackson	$14.99		
Two Mask One Heart 3 – Jacob Spears and Trayvon Jackson	$14.99		
Wrong Place Wrong Time – Silk White	$14.99		
Young Goonz – Reality Way	$14.99		
Subtotal:			
Tax:			
Shipping (Free) U.S. Media Mail:			
Total:			

Make Checks Payable To:
Good2Go Publishing
7311 W Glass Lane,
Laveen, AZ 85339